Ecstatic
Inferno

Fungasm Press

Portland + Los Angeles

PO Box 10065
Portland, OR 97296

ISBN: 978-1-62105-210-4

Copyright © 2015 by Autumn Christian

Cover Copyright © 2015 by Matthew Revert

Edited by John Skipp

Printed in the USA.

Ecstatic Inferno

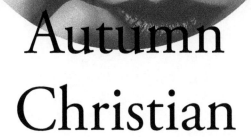

Autumn
Christian

Table of Contents

ON FICTION AS AN ALTERED STATE OF CONSCIOUSNESS (AND WHY THE BRAIN/SOUL OF AUTUMN CHRISTIAN IS MY NEW PSYCHOACTIVE SUBSTANCE OF CHOICE)

A WILD-EYED TESTIMONIAL INTRODUCTION BY JOHN SKIPP

I was born a haunted and wondering child. Can't remember a moment in which I wasn't. I knew I had landed in a very strange place. With no idea why.

God only knows what dreams I had.

But from the moment I was old enough to think, I wanted this world to spill its secrets. Was not content with rote, surface explanations for the wonders unfolding before me. Everyone around me treated this life as routine. Tried to teach me the rules, which seemed simple and clear. To them, at least.

But I was like, "Nope. Not even close."

There was something underneath that I needed to know.

Dr. Seuss was my first true ally in this quest. He made me fall in love with words, the symbols designed to explain it all. Expanded my nascent vocabulary one trillion percent.

Taught me rhythm and poetry. The joy of the dance. And tied the words to fantastical images that nailed them forever in my mind.

And oh, the images. Impossible visions. Doing things that the regular world couldn't or wouldn't, but which peeled back the meaning. Let me see under the skin.

At which point, he had altered my consciousness. Flipped the switch on my imagination gland. A switch that never went off, thank God or whatever, and became my default setting as I moved deeper into earthbound existence. Seeking out more, deeper truths and visions. A journey I continue to this day.

I bring all this up in the context of introducing the amazing Autumn Christian: another haunted child of wonder, currently blowing the lid off my mind. And now yours. You lucky bastard.

The easiest, quickest way in is to say that *Autumn Christian is the gene-splice baby of Philip K. Dick and Poppy Z. Brite.* And yes, that's exactly as good as it sounds.

But that ain't but the half of it.

Autumn's exquisite, reality-transformative prose combines all the flavor, rigor, nuance and pain of Poppy's best modern southern gothic brilliance with the incandescent off-the-charts visionary daring of 1960s New Wave science fiction, as popularized by Harlan Ellison's DANGEROUS VISIONS collections, and exemplified possibly best by Dick himself.

Flat-out: I'm a sucker for the fiction of ideas. The wilder the better. And *damn*, does she deliver! Be they futuristic (as in the extra-planetary heartbreaking nightmare classic "Honeycomb Heads", or the next-up-in-our-hideous-terrestrial-corporate-agenda-driven "They Promised Dreamless Death" and "Pink Crane Girls"), going extra-dimensional ("Out of the Slip Planet", "Your Demiurge Is Dead"), or just staggeringly mutating the here-and-now ("Crystalmouth", "Sunshine, Sunshine", "The Bad Baby Meniscus"), these stories consistently reach for and deliver such imaginative depths of thrilldom that my little child-brain shivers, trying to take it all in.

"The Dog That Bit Her" is the closest she comes to a monster we already think we know. But it ranks right up there with Violet LeVoit's "Warm, in Her Coat" as one of the god-damndest original spins on lycanthropy I have ever seen.

And honest to God, "The Singing Grass" (which closes this collection) brought me right to the fucking edge of a full-blown LSD flashback. I'm not kidding. I've never read a piece of prose that flipped my psychedelic trigger so hard. And I've read a lot of crazy shit.

Bottom line, and all comparisons aside, this Autumn Christian is truly one of a kind. Nobody else could have written such stories. Nobody else would have *even dared try*, much less actually pull them off in such immaculate fashion, creating her own brave new mythos in the process.

And as dark and weird and painful as her work most certainly gets, I couldn't believe how many times I laughed out loud at her stunning revelations and cunning turns of phrase. How much genuine literary wit slices through even the twistiest shit herein. Which is to say: this is not a grueling slog. It's – at least for me – a joyous one. Dare I say Fungasmic.

It's the kind of torch I'm proud to pass forward, lighting

the walls of the infinite tunnel for every gnostic seeker who ever hoped to part the veil. Peer beneath the surface. Whether you like what you find there or not.

That's pretty much all I ever wanted, from the moment I awoke into the dream that is this life. All the vast haunted wonder laid bare, in stunning barrages of unflinching honesty, jaw-droppingly poetic prose, and fiercely unbridled imagistic truth.

In short: I fucking love this book. Felt myself changed just by letting it into my brain. Not to mention my heart and soul.

And envy you the central-nervous-system-mutating revelatory trip you're about to take, right here on Earth.

Yer pal in the forever trenches,
Skipp

They Promised Dreamless Death

"Dear customer," the man on the television said, "no more twisting your spine and bracing hips in the night. Your restless weeks are wastelands of dissociative depression and existentialist boredom. You nurse the brink of destruction searching for rest. Let us into your mind; let us give you the dreamless and dark headspace you always wanted."

One by one my friends and family have disappeared under the gentle, slipwire cocoons of the machines. Mother's ghost smiled like a crooked dog. She hadn't been able to sleep, she told me, not after my father died, because that damn vampire stood at her bedside howling in her ear for the last twenty years. It didn't hurt, she told me when I asked, you don't feel anything at all.

I didn't know if it was really her speaking to me, from some netherworld of subconsciousness, or the machine the doctors placed in her head. Whatever it was, she assured me, that damn vampire was finally gone.

My brother tried to commit suicide his freshman year of college. Bipolar disorder, they said, little high little low. Years of therapy and medication could not diminish his slitwrists or gnashing teeth. How many undergraduate students, bent under the pressure of midterms and lovers that never call back, have gone into the dark woods and never returned? The machines promised relief. When he woke up in the next ten years, he would have graduated with a bachelor's degree, married a studious and slack-jawed maiden, had two kids, a great job, and absolutely no reason to be unhappy. Life would be better if we weren't present during our difficult transitory periods, if we shut off the part of us that thought and felt and tasted, and slid our heads down on dark waters while the machines lived for us.

I found him standing over my bed one night.

"It didn't hurt," my brother said, "you don't feel anything at all. This body doesn't sleep anymore. My head is blissfully unaware of the grief that's been transferred to my fingernails and my lips. Why don't you join me? You were always mother's favorite. What pressure, he said, what stress. Come and join me underwater in the long sleep. Five years, he said, fifteen, twenty, your life will be straightened out. You don't feel anything at all."

The next morning my mother made waffles and poached eggs, and my brother wrote in the margins of Notes from the Underground and drank cold coffee. The pink scars on his wrists from his suicide attempt were still visible, white in the middle, like soft, uncooked meat. There's no real difference in their personalities, their mannerisms. If I hadn't seen the machines inserted into them myself I would have thought nothing had changed. I just know that when mother pushes her hair out of her face and clips it in the back, or licks waffle batter off her finger, or when my brother roams the house during thunderstorms and types his college essays by the glow of the computer in the den, they are really creatures living dead, oblivious, sleeping heavy.

I remember when I was seventeen, before the machines came, and to my parents the only thing worse than death was being too alive. I couldn't tell them I drove my Camaro on the Texas backroads late at night with my girlfriend, drove to the place where Texas bottoms out, where the road is a glittering sink or swim, a fogged out dark shell melting everywhere the headlights didn't touch. Drove eighty miles an hour, ninety, a hundred, and my girlfriend, her name was Jeanine, all pretty girls were named Jeanine, she sat in the passenger seat looking at me softly biting her lip. I gripped the steering wheel and stared into the expanse of gloomy gray ahead, miles and miles of the ordinary world turned by the night into a Hades realm of shadow and ice.

I went up to a hundred and ten miles and death sat on the hood of the car, her hair blowing in the wind, her breasts pressed to the engine heat.

"Jeanine," I whispered.

Jeanine, the name for all pretty girls, the name for girls with parents who still think all their children are virgins. Jeanine, girl of my dreams, girl with my dick in her mouth. I couldn't stop the Camaro, couldn't slow, couldn't hesitate. I had to plaster every deer that stepped in the headlights and keep melting the asphalt with Jeanine's teeth and my foot on the pedal and her warm honey shy eyes in my stomach because I knew I'd never feel that way again.

I don't know how many people have succumbed to the machines, punched a hole in the living room or slit their skin to the bone and said, this is enough for me, slip it under. It's illegal to release machine records; they're under the strictest confidence and security, just like adoption records. It's illegal to discriminate against those who have the machine, not that employers or employees would ever know. Only the closest family and friends are aware when you decide to let doctors insert the machine into your head. I don't know how many people I know are sleeping dead, consciousness and subconsciousness slipped into the warm, insidious cradle of the machine's rocket. Life is too cruel, the man on the television says, for us to live it ourselves.

Mother's ghost smiled at me when she came down the stairs and entered the kitchen. I sat at the kitchen table with my open document of empty words and a cup of coffee and I watched her face. If I cut her she would cry, but inside, where the heart and head lived, she wouldn't feel a thing. If I killed her it would just be an exchange of one darkness for another. She'd never rise again. She'd never know. She poured herself a cup of coffee and looked out the window into the blue garden. I love the sunshine, she said, we never get to see the sunshine anymore. I said nothing. She turned toward me.

"I love you," she said.

"Yeah, whatever Mom," I said, putting down the knife, "I love you too."

When it got dark I drove to the strip club downtown. I sat in a machinated box, electrified myself with blazing blue and orange lights, paid for three seven dollar beers, cheap American shit, too, and I waited for Boxy November to come on stage. Boxy colored her hair like the lights, orange at the tips, blue up to the roots. She rose up on stage like sleek, sleek metal, PVC boots click click clicking, silver brassiere shining, thong slung low tongue wet. She flung her dirty hair back, sunk, unclasped her brassiere, and I knew she was the only woman worth living for anymore. I knew she'd never let the machines inside her head.

"Suicide rates are down by 46% percent," the man on the television said.

My brother continued to stand at the foot of my bed advertising for the machines in the hours when he used to sleep.

"Come and join us," he said, like some phantom whispering fang-seductive from the other side of the living dead railroad tracks. "We have several easy payment plans for your evisceration. We take all major credit cards. All your friends are doing it. What do you really have to offer the world in your consciousness anyways? Nobody will miss you. Why is it so difficult for you to acquiesce, sir? Are you following some self-righteous religious creed, sir? Is that why you can't suck it up, lay back, and blow your head out of the water, sir?"

I think that while the world is sleeping a new entity will enter our universe, like a thief in the night, creep over our head-fog, and take away our bodies and our space, infiltrate our energy and our nightmarescapes. If the world ever wakes, I don't think it will ever know what it used to be.

Boxy November told me once after hours that she was sure the machines were going to turn us all into morticians and taxidermists.

"Dark energy doesn't just disappear," she said, "doesn't just kick its legs out like a dog and go to sleep. It's probably working in the back of all those zombie brains, she said.

"What? I said.

"You know, the dark energy," she said, "do you want to go back to your place?"

"I don't want to wake my mother," I said.

"She's a deadhead, isn't she?" Boxy asked.

I didn't reply.

"She is," Boxy said. Sighed. Her fingers twitched. She was trying to quit smoking. Ten years of it had stretched out her face, turned her soft honey eyes into droopy dog wells, cut the frown lines of her mouth too heavy for makeup to cover.

"Lets go to your car," she said, and once we were in the car and the doors were locked and the ignition turned on she said, "let's drive, like we used to."

"No," I said, "I can't."

Fifteen years had wasted the both of us, widened our eyes, lopped off our fingers, unraveled our skin. She was Boxy November now, the only woman worth living for anymore, a woman naked and without ambition, dead like all women, dead even without the machines inside her head, and I, dead alongside her, our two corpses propped up in my Camaro just dying for another cigarette. We weren't pretty people anymore. That's why she had to change her name, strip, press her dry mouth to the wet faucet, why she wasn't Jeanine anymore, the name for all pretty girls, why she never let me call her Jeanine anymore.

I couldn't even get it up anymore.

"How many more years do you have before they take

the machines out of you?" I asked my brother.

The machines had turned all of our heads into a landscape of dark eyes, sloping giant hills, shadows of the valley of death. Metaphysics told us the world didn't exist without being observed. Dead inside our heads, the machines chuk-chuk-chuking, the silent whirr pressing the consciousness in the back, to a dreamless land, we were turning our world into a world for locusts. We were making the universe blind.

"Ten more years," he said, "I'm going to become a taxidermist."

I sat up in bed and laughed and laughed and stuffed my mouth into my pillow and laughed.

I was seventeen years old again, and Jeanine wanted to go to Nevada. My Camaro broke down in the desert and we spent the night on the top of the car, looking up at the stars burning up, rationing the water. In the morning I worked on fixing the car. The heat bent my head. I saw an angel's halo in the sunlight, an angel stretching her fingers into sunrays and setting the warped cone of the desert on fire. Jeanine wandered around the desert, her hair tied up at the top of her head, her sweat swelling up, the color of a heartbeat. I took a break from trying to fix the car and went out searching for her. I found a rattlesnake sleeping in the bleached white of a cow's skull. I shook the rattlesnake out with a stick and picked up the cows skull, hugged it to my chest.

I found Jeanine shortly after.

"We're going to die," I said.

"So I guess you haven't fixed the car." Jeanine said.

"No."

"We're not going to die. Don't be silly."

"This died," I said. I cradled the skull like a baby.

"Everything dies," she said, "but not us. Not today."

"Why not today?" Seems like a good a day as any."

"I think you may be a little bit delirious," she said, "give me the skull."

"No. I like it. It's mine."

"We're not going to die, okay?" she said. "Not today."

"Why?"

"Because next summer we're going to go to a lake. A wonderful, glittering, sparkling, cool lake, and we're going to forget there was this horrible heat, and we're going to swim out so far we can't touch the bottom. We can't go to the lake if we die. We're going to the lake," she said, "so we're not going to die."

In my dreams sometimes, when I can manage to sleep, my brother is out in that desert with us, and he is sitting on the ground, the sunlight refusing to touch his head. There is a dark space around his eyes, like a black hole sucking out the features of his face. Behind him is a valley of glazed eyed stuffed animals, dogs and cats and cattle, a legion of taxidermist creations.

"Dark energy," he said, "Boxy was right, brother, you never escape the forces inside of you, you just subvert them, make them change shape. I'm going to stuff a black bear next. We have several easy payment plans for your evisceration. We take all major credit cards. They're my favorite, the black bears."

I drove to the clinic. I filled out all the forms in the crowded waiting room, surrounded by so many people waiting to be turned into zombies, so many people desperate for one good night's sleep. When the nurse called for me I got up and she led me through an endless hallway of rooms. All the rooms were bleached white, white as bones, and it gave the building this aura of perpetual space, this inevitability. I looked into every room. I almost passed one room and then, when I saw who was inside, stopped in its doorway.

"Sir, we need to keep moving," said the nurse.

"No," I said, "No. See, I know this woman."

Inside the room Boxy November lay on a steely surgical table while doctors took the machine out of her head.

"Sir," the nurse said, "sir."

"I don't want the operation anymore," I said, "leave me alone."

The nurse left. I stood outside the room and watched Boxy and the doctors. The machine came out of her head shiny, ichor dark, glittering with her blood. It curled like a spider, silver points tipped with hot iron. Boxy breathed mechanically. The doctors placed the machine in a toxic waste receptacle. I watched her come out of her sleep in stages. When one of the doctors left the room, I grabbed his arm.

"Is she going to be okay?" I asked.

"Oh yes," he said, "but sometimes when people come out of the sleep, they're very disoriented. You know, they feel cold."

I let him go.

Boxy came out of the room in a white hospital gown, her orange and blue hair unwashed and damp against her head. She rubbed her bare arm with her palm, squeezed.

"Why are you here?" she asked.

"I'm here for you," I said, "how do you feel?"

"Tired," she said. "I want to take a nap."

We left the clinic. I drove.

"They said when I woke up I would be in love," she said.

"You are," I said.

"What happened to my hair?" she asked.

"We can fix that later."

"Where are we going?"

I didn't respond. The light, that harsh angel light, suffused the car. Boxy fell asleep against the car door, her hair plastered to the window. I rolled down my window. The warm air rustled her hospital gown, touched her limp wrists. We left the city and entered a near-abandoned countryside. I pushed the car up to ninety miles per hour, a hundred, a hundred and ten. The sun's shadow came up out of the valley. I drove to the nearest lake. I hadn't been to the lake since I was six years old, and it was smaller than I remembered. It cupped the sun in its head and shimmered a softer green-blue.

"Wake up," I said to Boxy, "we're here."

"I just want to sleep," she said, "let's go home."

"You've been sleeping for years, Boxy," I said.

"Boxy?" she asked. "Who's Boxy?"

"Jeanine," I said, "I mean Jeanine."

We get out of the car.

"Why are we here?" Jeanine asked.

"I never got to take you to that lake," I said, "you know, after the desert."

"We broke up," she said.

"I know, but now we're here," I said.

We walked to the pier. We were the only ones at the lake, us and the sun, dipping low to heat the water, and Jeanine stood at the edge of the pier in her hospital gown, the ties teased by the wind.

"You don't have a machine in you, do you? Jeanine asked. She turned toward me.

"No," I said. "I was going to get one, but something made me stop."

"What made you stop?" she asked.

She turned back toward the water, reached behind her and untied the strings of her hospital gown. It fluttered around her hips and she caught it in one hand, held it out over the water, blue and orange hair blown off her neck, hospital gown struggling like a butterfly. I could count every vertebrate on her back, touch the shoulder blades protracting like wings.

"I don't know," I said.

"Deadhead," she said.

She let the hospital gown go. It flew out of her hands and dropped into the water. She jumped into the lake.

The sun lit my fingers. I took off my shirt and jumped in the waters after Jeanine, into the place where light overtakes the dark.

Crystalmouth

We saw a ghost in the corner of the room. Hard black poison. Porcelain fingers and teeth set in six rows. He never slept. He scratched the floor in our dreams. He unlatched the window to let the cool air in so we couldn't get warm. Momma said, "no ghosts here. No ghosts since the last exorcism," but she was superstitious like that. She'd been superstitious ever since her mother smeared blackberry and hemlock on her belly and we came out of her slippery blue and stuck together.

We are Craniopagus conjoined siblings. Conjoined sisters. Siamese twins. That means in the womb our skulls fused together. The nurse tried to smother my smaller sister because she didn't know any better. My sister ghost-haired and octopus-limbed. She clung to me screaming and screaming until they dragged the nurse away.

It means we dream the same dreams.

It means we saw the same ghost, no matter how many

exorcists our mother hired. He dragged his toes against the hardwood floor. His claws clickened and clackened. We clung to each other. His mouth stretched. Heavy. Yawning. Burrowing, big mouth. Big tongue. Crystals studded his tongue. They shredded the roof of his mouth so that the skin hung down in thick strips, and when he breathed the strips fluttered.

Each night he came a little closer to the bed. My sister threw salt down on the floor but he stepped right over it. Clicken. Clacken. The crystals grew heavy in his mouth, and when he unlatched the window they sparkled in darklight. My sister's snowpowder hair fell off the bed and he bent down and wound it around his wrists to drag himself closer to us.

She said, "This wouldn't have happened to anyone else."

"Don't talk like that," I said, but as always, she was probably right.

"You're lucky," the doctors told our mother, "most Craniopagus siblings come out stillborn."

The doctors told our mother that they could separate us. My sister would die, of course. She's smaller, the parasitic twin, growth stunted in the womb because I'm greedy. Greedy. But our mother could only shake her head and speak like a gasp.

"No. No."

I feel sorry for our mother: only 22 years old when she birthed her mutant. I can see her in the hospital bed cradling her new child, that eight limbed with a swelling head. She's a mousy fern of a girl with a deadbeat dad and a religious father with what looks like God's strident vengeance spilled into her lap and all she can think is,

"I only bought clothes for one baby."

Autumn Christian

She took us home unsplit and fed us and clothed us. Even when her mother, poison alchemist, tried to put arsenic in our pudding, rat-poison in our milk formula. Killing us would have been her special delight. I imagine she wanted to dip us in formaldehyde and nail us to a piece of wood to sell to a curio shop. Or to take revenge on her daughter for not dying in her womb after she drank wormwood tea and ingested parsley and rotten berries and Vitamin C. After she screamed "Out! Out!" like performing an exorcism, after throwing herself down the stairs.

Yet our mother lived. And we lived. Me and my pale rasping sister. We lived.

And we grew. When we were six years old we played marbles in the woods out behind the house, the two of us splayed out in the dirt and our eyes oriented toward the trees, beaded sweat dripping from my cheek to hers. Another neighborhood child, little Thomas, stumbled into our clearing and screamed when he saw us. Tears sprang to his eyes. Hot and wild tears. He started running in circles because he couldn't find the way out. He tripped over our marbles and fell in the dirt.

My sister laughed.

"Don't do that," I said.

She couldn't help herself. She laughed and laughed, and this only caused Thomas to scratch harder at the dirt, to press his hands into his cherub curls and tear out patches. My sister grabbed at his ankle. He screamed louder. I slapped her hand. He scrambled to his feet and ran off into the trees, vine scratches on his face.

"You shouldn't have done that," I said.

And though I couldn't look at her face with our heads

20

fused together, I felt the muscles in my head tense as she smiled.

"It's fun," she said, "to be a monster sometime."

As the ghost crept closer to the bed, my sister wouldn't let me sleep. She tugged on my hair at the nape of my neck. She scratched my skin.

I grabbed at her stomach. I slapped the side of her face.

"Stop it," I said, "stop."

"It's not a ghost. It's an incubus."

"How do you know?" I asked, my head pressed to the sheets, jaw pasted to the wall.

In the periphery of my vision the ghost - incubus - stared at the wall with a blankless stare. His mouth heaved. Underneath his skin his organs glowed. A faint, blue glow.

"I read about it," she said.

She kicked the sheets off the bed.

I turned and tossed in bed, my legs catching chill. But when I brushed up against my sister she's burning up. Her skin cooking on the surface, skinny little legs flushed red. She panted with her teeth twisting in her mouth.

The incubus could almost reach over and brush her toes with his fingers now. Bend over and snap them off.

"Go away," I whispered to the incubus.

I shivered as the cool air blew through the window.

I shivered but my sister's hot hot hot.

Our teachers told us we could be anyone we wanted. Doctor. Scientist. Stripper. I was always the studious type, but my sister preferred to roll in the grass, blow bubbles into a child's mouth. I imagined myself trying to perform open-heart surgery with my head twisted to the ceiling and a lopsided blue mask slipping off my nose. I saw my sister welded to me, pregnant and laughing and shaking my surgeon's knife. In my dreams she released butterflies in the operating room. Wove a spider's net into my hair.

No, I couldn't be a doctor. We couldn't be doctors. We'd read the books about people like us; we'd visited the websites. Chang and Eng Bunker, the conjoined twins from Thailand that performed in P.T. Barnum's circus. Millie and Christine McCoy, or "The Two-Headed NIghtingale," conjoined slave children taught to sing and dance for money, stolen away in the night like a toy. Daisy and Violet Hilton, performed in movies like Freaks and Chained for Life. Died alone in their apartment, passing bad blood from one to the other.

They may chain us to the floor or give us a violin or open our mouths and climb inside, but it doesn't change anything. We can never be anything but Craniopagus conjoined siblings. Conjoined sisters. Siamese twins.

I know this because once my sister fell in love. Some deadhead marijuana mouthed boy who thought he had a savior complex until he met us. He climbed over our fence from a nearby party, drunk and laughing to himself. We were outside on the porch alone, drinking our virgin margaritas that our mother made for us, pursing our sour lips.

"I know you," he said, "you're the twins everyone talks about."

He crawled across the grass in the dew toward us.

"You're the pretty one," he said to my sister.

Of course he would think that of my parasite. She was the glass skinned Ophelia sprung from my head. The girl with the kind of stunted limbs usually only seen in dead anorexics and jellyfish on the bottom of the sea.

"You don't know what pretty is," I said.

"Can I have a drink?" he asked my sister, ignoring me.

"It's virgin," she said, and for some reason this made both of them laugh.

She held the drink out to him and he spilled it on his chin. It dripped down onto his shirt. They laughed and laughed.

Someone called for the boy over the fence. He scrambled up, knocking the glass out of my sister's hand, and ran.

After that night he sent my sister little lace and sugar messages hidden in the trees out in the forest. He tied candied pecans and tiny teddy bears to balloons that floated through our window.

"You look so happy," our mother said to her.

"She thinks she's in love," I said.

My sister touched the lace heart that he'd wedged underneath the door. She stroked her snowpowder hair.

"Let her think that then," our mother said.

"Fine. I won't ruin her fantasy then."

"What's gotten into you? Why talk to your sister like that?"

And as my mother strained over the kitchen sink, trying to rub the leprous spots off her hand, I thought: because maybe I wanted to be a doctor. Because maybe I wanted to go to sleep for once knowing that my dreams belonged only to me.

"She doesn't get to fall in love," I said.

I went back to bed hauling my parasite.

One morning a matted, lean stray cat dropped down the hallway window and came screeching down to our bedroom. We jumped out of bed. My sister caught the cat in-between her knees. Around its neck we found a string with a letter attached.

Party at my house. Wednesday night. Dress pretty.

She demanded a dress. Silver. Peach ribbons. A pearl necklace. Something that could be zipped up in the back, We had to shop in the child's section of the department store, with the children and their mother's staring at us blank-faced and wounded for life. When she picked out her dress we stood together in front of the triple-way mirror. Three monsters. Three lady trolls grimacing and mad.

She tugged at the ends of her hair. She smoothed out the silver dress.

"I could almost..."

"Almost what?"

"Feel like I was real. A real girl."

"Pretend like I wasn't here, you mean"

"That's not it. That's not it."

At the party I refused to drink but became drunk anyways, because the boys kept feeding my sister drinks. They smoked her out and my head went sluggish and slow. The boy stroked her hair, told her that he loved her. We went into a back room with my brain crumbling. I ached to fall asleep. It'd been so long since I slept. My sister giggled shy as he led us onto the bed.

"Undress for me," she said.

"He'll break you," I said, laughing as the room spun, "you're just a little parasite."

She slapped me on the nose. The cheek. The boy panted as he unbuckled his pants and he stepped out of them with skinny, breakable legs

That's when I noticed the ghost in the corner of the room. Another incubus, I thought. They're everywhere these days. Becoming immune to the exorcisms, probably. If only we hadn't exorcised those demons from the bedsheets and the baby crib, the staircase and the water glass. If only our grandma hadn't rubbed hemlock on my mother's belly, then maybe the demons wouldn't be here now.

The incubus dragged himself closer to the bed. He didn't have a crystal mouth or a glowing rotten seed for a belly or porcelain skin. He had dirty fingernails and a baseball cap and a t-shirt that smelled of whiskey.

The lover boy lowered himself onto my sister. He wound knots into her hair. They kissed.

"Hey," I said, all I could manage to say, a whiskey slur.

They ignored me.

"Hey, does anyone else see that?"

The boy-disguised-as-incubus jumped onto me. He smashed his lips against my jaw and the room tilted on its side. I thought we'd fall off the side of the bed, with his tennis shoes digging into my pelvis and his hunch-limbed spine hitting the seaside portrait above our heads.

My sister smashed a lamp over his head, spraying him and me with glass. Incubus boy fell off me laughing. Lover boy jumped off my sister wiping at his mouth.

She picked up her torn party dress and we fled.

"I didn't know," she said as we limped back home.

We left behind pieces of silver, tattered pieces of her dress, pieces of glass. By the time we got to the porch our legs were about to break. We quivered with the strain. My sister tried to keep from crying but I felt her tears drip onto my shoulder. So hot they nearly burned through my skin.

We dragged ourselves up the stairs, our mother asleep down the hall.

"Do you know what an incubus does?" my sister said, tugging on my hair.

"Please," I said, "I just want to sleep."

"He steals your energy."

"Please."

"He fucks you while you sleep."

We fell into bed and the incubus waited in his usual spot. She choked like she couldn't breathe. My heart pounded with the sudden rush of blood from her to me. In the dark my fingers tiptoed over the wasteland of her stomach.

"Him?" I said. "He won't. "We're more of a monster than he'll ever be."

I opened my mouth and hissed. My sister tried to laugh but only rasped. The incubus tapped his toes against the floor. Clicken. Clacken.

In the morning we lay on the couch shell-shocked and half dressed. One sock for four feet. Sweaters with split buttons. Our mother sat cross-legged on the carpet with a book of demonology in her lap. A thick, black leather bound tome of a book. She was seeing curses everywhere again: little runic prints on our arms and faces. Maybe she even saw the brand of the incubus like a dark crystal hovering over us.

If only we'd been born real twins, Momma, without this piece of skull sewn between us. Maybe then the incubus wouldn't have come. Maybe lover boy wouldn't have brought his friend into the room to rape me while he made love to my pale ectoplasm of a sister. I could have been a doctor.

"I'm sorry, girls," our mother said, because she could see

the scratches on my face where the glass sprayed against me, because she'd found the tattered remains of my sister's silver dress stuffed into the trashcan.

"Don't be," I said, "it's not like you weren't expecting it."

Our mother hummed underneath her breath - some ritual incantation.

"Don't worry, Momma. It won't happen again."

In that moment I could see every place she'd ever been hurt. I saw the broken stem cells in her belly, the way my sister and me sought each other out in the darkness of her. I saw the scars that tattooed her back where her father struck her with belt-straps, the place where the dog bit her as a child and she screamed and screamed but no one came.

She stretched out on the carpet until her face almost touched the floor, the book underneath her stomach. I reached out for her. I was so tired, everything out of proportion. She seemed a thousand years away.

"It won't happen again," I said.

In the night the incubus unlatched the window.

He crawled onto the bed. He opened his mouth and the crystals bulged heavy on his tongue. They glowed fiercer than I ever remembered before. So bright, that tears sprung to my eyes to look at him. He heaved and I shivered. My sister melted down into the sheets. She couldn't breathe in the heat.

I tried to throw off the sheets and run, but I couldn't move. The air pressed down with an unbearable heaviness. My lungs welded themselves into my chest. I couldn't scream for my mother. I couldn't whisper help. Help me.

The incubus lowered himself onto my sister, puffs of shadow for arms. He ripped my sister's dress apart with his studded tongue. The shredded skin on the roof of his mouth spilled out on her bare stomach like pale ribbons. I wanted to close my eyes, but I couldn't.

I'm so sorry, my sister. I'm so sorry. I wanted to give you love but I can't even turn my head. You can let butterflies into my operating room, sister. You can fall in love. Please, sister.

Sister, please don't let us disappear.

Through the darkness my sister reached out and held my hand.

The spell broke. She grabbed the incubus by the throat and pulled him closer.

"Come here," she whispered to me, her tongue in his mouth, "come here."

The fever could have burst her brain. My hands sizzled on the back of her hands. We fell backwards into the sheets, hit our head on the baseboards. Kept falling. Spinning, until we were nauseous, his breath distorting space, our heads.

Something. A little something inside of me
stirred.

I touched the cool place on the back of the incubus' head. I touched his shadows for arms.

"Come here," I whispered.

We wrapped our legs around him. Our bare legs touched on his back, hot and cold. We rolled him onto his back, pressed him down. We stretched our spines and rolled our hips.

We tossed our hair back.

The incubus squirmed beneath us with his mouth unable to be closed. The crystals grew and grew until his tongue throbbed. We grabbed his arms and wrestled him to the floor, the three of us a worn pile of bodies, our limbs indistinguishable from him to us.

"I told you we were monsters," I said to the incubus

I didn't feel cold anymore.

My sister reached inside his mouth and grabbed his tongue, studded with crystals. He started choking. He heaved and heaved. She reached in with her other hand. Pulled.

The incubus collapsed underneath us. My sister opened her hands and his crystal tongue studded thudded to the floor. The dark disappeared.

The incubus squirmed underneath us, unable to scream. Rasping, without his crystal tongue. The heaviness in my chest left me. I could breathe again.

We grappled him to the floor.

Maybe our mother would find us in the morning on the floor, melted into the hips of a demon. Three instead of two. Or she'd find us worn down to the bone with the light burning a hole through our ends. Either way we'd be laughing. Laughing.

I didn't know where I ended and she began. I touched her hips and wondered why I'd gone numb. My head ached in the back, my skull trying to reach around and escape.

I don't know if we'll stay together forever like this, torn-fused Kali monster, or if we'll tear each other apart.

Your Demiurge is Dead

It's been forty nights since Jehovah washed up on the Gulf of Mexico in three black trash-bags. After that, the Triple Goddess showed up at the White House and announced to a live television audience of thirty million that a new era had begun. This was right about the same time I answered an emergency call at four that morning and went down to Mimi's trailer where she lived with a catatonic white boyfriend and twelve children. I pulled her oldest daughter dead out from the fennel in the backyard where she slit her wrists and lay down to die.

"I raised my kids better than that," Mimi said, as my partner Thatch and I zipped up her daughter's already-blue corpse into a body bag. The remaining children, who had Mimi's dull green feral eyes and slack faces, hovered close to me.

"I can make you some sweet tea before you go," Mimi said.

"Goddamn it woman," Mimi's boyfriend, whom I only knew as the boyfriend, called from his recliner, "nobody wants your goddamn sweet tea."

"We're very busy tonight, Mimi," I said, "as you can see." I indicated the body bag.

"Perhaps some other time, then. Come on kids, it's past your bedtime," she said.

But the children followed me out to where my police cruiser and an ambulance waited on the street.

The paramedic was asleep in the front seat of the ambulance. Thatch and I put the girl's body in the back.

When I turned around there the children were, silent and sharp-faced in the dark.

"Are you married?" one of the girls asked Thatch. She was about sixteen years old, sick-skinny, with white hair like a powdered Christmas tree.

"Yep," Thatch said, "twelve years now."

She turned to me. "What is your name?" she asked. "Are you married?"

"Officer Redding," I said. "And no."

"Why not?" she asked.

I looked over at Thatch. He shrugged. I looked back over at the girl, her brothers and sisters surrounding her like she was a satellite while they made hunger eyes and bit their hands.

"I don't like the thought of someone else having a say in what I do or who I am," I said.

"All relationships are about control," she said. "What's your first name, Officer Redding? My name's Tuesday."

"I'm sorry, we don't really have time for this," I said.

"It's Bill," Thatch said.

"My sister didn't kill herself," Tuesday said.

"What do you mean?"

"Will you marry me under the dogwood tree, Bill? Julie wanted to be married under the dogwood tree. We were all so mad at Julie. She was going to leave us and she was the only one who took care of us."

"Tuesday, what do you mean your sister didn't kill herself?"

I looked over at Thatch again. He was on his cell phone text-messaging someone, while there we were, surrounded by twelve children and empty Oklahoma farmland. The night rose like smoke. The stars and half-moon sliced off the ends of our fingers. I heard nothing but the children's slow dance breath and my ribcage breaking and Thatch's phone going click-click-click.

Tuesday moved toward me and I realized how tall she was, taller than me or Thatch, her bones a church ceiling.

"Did you know God died this week?" she whispered, her lips electric against my forehead.

"Yes," I said.

"The preacher says God is inside all of us, but Momma said only rich people get to be God. I think she might be right."

"Did someone kill your sister, Tuesday?" I asked.

She grabbed my hair in her fist and pulled my head back. She kissed me on the forehead.

"That's all you're going to get," she said, "until after we're married."

She released me. I jerked back and hit my head on the ambulance. Thatch continued to text-message.

Click click click. Tuesday and the children fled into the dark and disappeared, as if swallowed by a thick, black-tongued wave. I woke the paramedic up by banging on the window and dragged Thatch to the squad car.

"I think we might have a murder case," I said as I drove back into town. "You heard what that girl said, didn't you, Thatch?"

"Who would murder one of Mimi's poor, white-trash children? That girl was just messing with you."

When I got back home I couldn't sleep so I watched late-night news. They were still showing the footage from when the Triple Goddess went to the White House. Everyone in America knew the country belonged to the gods, and not the politicians, but nobody really knew what to think of this new era. The Triple Goddess was a stunner, no doubt, wearing six-inch heels and cruel shadows, walking across the White House lawn in the same dresses that Angelina Jolie wore at the Grammy's. She had tall, severe bodies, because Cosmo said the most successful women were the tallest, and the most beautiful, but she was a goddess and the bodies couldn't look too innocent, or welcoming, and could only be sexual in the most alien way.

"Now that the demiurge is dead," she said into the microphones with her brass, slow-over-the-water voices, "we will see vast improvements in the quality of life in this country. I've already drawn up a nationwide health care plan for the middle class, as well as a plan for several new worship centers to be built in forty-four states."

Everyone knew the Triple Goddess killed Jehovah. There were three bodies of the incarnate, all-

Supreme Being. There were three trash bags of summer-heated, red exposed fetid god flesh that washed up on the Gulf of Mexico. It couldn't get much more dark and symbolic than that. She tore Jehovah apart, probably while He was out on his pontoon shark fishing, and then made sure America knew He wasn't in charge anymore

The station received another emergency call from Mimi's trailer. A domestic abuse call. Thatch and I drove out there in the tar dark.

"Fuck," Thatch said while we were on the road, "no cellphone service here. And they say nationwide coverage."

I said nothing.

"The Triple Goddess is going to start regulating the cell phone companies. So they'll stop ripping people off. That's what I heard."

"That's nice," I said.

Thatch and I drove up to Mimi's trailer. All the children were out in the yard, and I had to slam on the brakes to keep from driving over Mimi as she ran across the street chasing her boyfriend with a metal meat tenderizer.

"Goddamn it," Thatch said.

I got out of the squad car. Tuesday ran around to my side of the car.

"What's going on here?" I asked her. She'd been the one who made the call.

"Momma and her boyfriend got into a fight again," she said.

Thatch took out across the road and into the empty field after Mimi and her boyfriend, one hand on his gun holster. He got about halfway across the field before he caught up with Mimi. Thatch tackled her and went down in the sick yellow grass with Mimi on top of him, her flailing her limbs in the air. The boyfriend was still running across the field, thinking Mimi was still following him. Thatch wrested

Mimi underneath him and pried the meat tenderizer out of her hand. Mimi tried to scratch Thatch's face. He grabbed her wrists and pulled them above her head. It was about this time the boyfriend realized he wasn't being chased anymore, turned around, and screamed across the field, "Yeah, teach that bitch a lesson!"

I moved to help Thatch. Tuesday reached out and took my wrist.

"It'll be okay," she said. "Momma gets tired easy. Don't arrest her; I just wanted you to scare some sense into her. It's been like this all day."

"That's not protocol," I said. "We get a disturbance call like this, we can't just leave."

I pulled my wrist away from Tuesday's grasp. I turned back toward the field.

Tuesday moved fast, grabbed my arm.

"Bill," she said.

I looked back at her. She was bent down toward me, her spine twisted, the bones of her face and limbs hard and struck with half-light from the dog-tongued moon, and when she tilted her head and stared at me I saw right through her feral green eyes, right straight through, into that sticky hollow place where all wounded children lived. I knew this place. A place called, my Daddy left me before I could say goodbye, I live with a mother that doesn't even exist, a place called, please don't leave me.

"Bill," she said again, "please don't arrest her."

Thatch took Mimi back through the field and across the street to where the children waited on the lawn. We calmed down Mimi and her boyfriend and then we left.

"Hey Bill," Thatch said on the way back to the station,

through the fog-black tar road, "did you notice there was only eleven children outside?"

"What? What do you mean only eleven?"

"I only counted eleven outside," he said, "and I remember there being twelve."

"Maybe one of them was around back, or inside the trailer," I said, but when I said it my stomach bottomed out and I knew it wasn't true.

"Hey, my wife Linda, you remember her, right?" Thatch said. "Well, she met a prophet of the Triple Goddess a few days ago and he invited us to dinner. You want to come along?"

I laughed.

"I'm serious," he said, "Linda says this guy is legit. I mean, he's a little strange, but all prophets are, you know, that's part of their charm."

"A prophet. In this damn town," I said.

"Just tell me if you want to go. Linda says she wants you to go."

Linda, I thought. Christ. The name for all blank-faced, beat-poor wives. The name for those who make cherry pies and wear aprons in the summertime.

"Bill," Thatch said to get my attention.

"Yeah," I said, "yeah, whatever, I'll go."

The prophet of the Triple Goddess lived a few miles out of town beside a silo wrecked by an F-5 hurricane and a trash pit filled with Grandma's furniture and glass Coke bottles warped flat by the heat. The prophet drove a Kia with a bumper sticker plastered on the back that read, "I'll give up my gun when you pry it from my cold dead fingers." He also had a lot of white, ragged-eared cats. Thatch and

I, and Linda, dressed in a pink dress with ruffles and click-click-click heels, walked up to the door.

"Knock," I told Thatch.

"You do it," he said.

I looked back and Linda was bending over petting one of the gnarled cats.

I knocked on the door.

The prophet of the Triple Goddess was forty pushing fifty, with a pepper-colored comb-over and a sagging body. He wore a wife-beater and green camouflage pants, T-shades and a wooden Buddhist prayer necklace, a mala, wound around one wrist. One of the cats tried to run into the house and he nudged it away with his foot.

"Come inside," he said, his face slack. "I ordered Pizza Hut."

So Linda, Thatch, the prophet, and I sat around the prophet's cramped kitchen table eating pepperoni pizza off of blue china and drinking chardonnay from coffee mugs. The walls were covered with writing in an indecipherable language. When Linda got up to go to the bathroom she had to walk through a maze of notebooks and stacks of computer paper.

"So, why did the Triple Goddess choose you?" Thatch asked the prophet.

Because I am nothing without her," he said.

"It's strange," I said, "that the Triple Goddess of America chooses you as a prophet, when you live out in the middle of fucking nowhere."

"I get to travel," he said. "Next month I'm going to Oklahoma City."

"Tell me how the Triple Goddess chose you," Thatch

said. "I'm curious. I'm genuinely curious."

Thatch and I exchanged looks. Linda was still in the bathroom.

"I found the Triple Goddess in a bottle of honey," he said, "do you want to see it? I still have the bottle. It looks like a bear. The bottle does."

"I didn't know she could fit inside a bottle of honey," Thatch said.

"The Triple Goddess is everywhere," the prophet said.

"Then why does she stick herself in a honey bottle?" Thatch said, "doesn't make much sense if you ask me."

The prophet's neck became splotchy red. He had dull, lizard eyes. I shouldn't have been scrutinizing him so closely. I wasn't one to judge who the gods made into their prophets. The gods loved ugly people. Muhammad and John Smith and Moses and Elijah and L. Ron Hubbard were chosen, I think, because of it. Because they were simply strange. Everybody would believe in a prophet who had straight teeth and a pediatric degree and made love to his wife on a regular schedule. It took real faith to believe in these sick and crooked-fingered misanthropes.

Linda came back from the bathroom.

"Hey sweetie," Thatch said, "our host was just telling us about how he became a prophet of the Triple Goddess."

Linda sat down and tried to look interested.

"Well," the prophet continued, "she was in this honey bottle, right. And when I twisted open the lid she called me from the depths, straight to the bottom, and a pink light shone all around me, blinding me. She said, 'from these depths, I have chosen you. Just as I have come to you through the sweetness of honey, so will I make your words sweet to the people. You are to write for me a gospel that will be read for the next two thousand years.' I must have passed out after that, because I woke up on the kitchen floor and all those damn cats were on top of me."

"Fascinating," Linda said.

I looked out the nearby window. From across about an acre of deadwood and trash I saw Mimi's trailer.

"Hey, I didn't realize you lived so close to Mimi," I said.

"Oh, Mimi," the prophet said. "Yeah, we grew up together. We're good friends."

I said nothing.

"I mean, we used to be. As you can see, I have a lot of work to do, so I don't have much time for visitors. Or a romantic relationship. You understand," the prophet said.

"Of course," Thatch said. I saw him roll his eyes.

"But, you know, the Goddess doesn't say I have to be completely abstinent. Since She is now inside of me I no longer get sick. My seed is special. Blessed. I could impregnate your wife if you wanted."

Linda tightened her hands on her napkin and looked down. I looked down at my plate.

"I thought you said the Triple Goddess was in everyone," Thatch said, "that She was everywhere. So why would you be any more special than anyone else?"

"Because She's inside of me more than you," the prophet said.

And I thought, dear dead God, he actually believes what he says. He believes that inside this sallow, pudding skin and heat-heavy face lives a special divinity. Something struck him in the face from a honey bottle, that saved him from influenza and diphtheria, that pushes its way through his sperm, that turns his fingers into matchsticks to fill papers and papers and then the walls when he's run out of paper, something that asphyxiates him in the night hours with its presence, and yet, something that, despite all the desire to be powerful and grandiose and important, is still so horribly mundane.

"I'm so sorry," Linda said to me on the way back home. She rode up in the front seat with Thatch, and turned around to talk to me in the back. "I had no idea he would be like that." "It's all right, he didn't offer to impregnate me, Linda," I said.

Thatch laughed. Linda laughed nervously.

"I just don't know what to think of all of this," Linda said. "This Triple Goddess, the death of Jehovah. It's such a scandal."

"We're just repeating history, babe," Thatch said, "cyclic life and death, karma dharma, whatever, it's all the same damn thing."

"Well I don't believe that," Linda said. "I refuse to believe that we're just like – like animals running on a track."

"Refuse it all what you want," Thatch said. "Reality isn't going away anytime soon."

When I went back home and lay in bed I knew that back in Mimi's trailer a tall frail girl with white hair and feral eyes and cricket bones lay down between ten brothers and sisters sleeping like dogs. Her eyes were open, limbs collapsed and breathed upon. She waited in the dark for the windows to scratch, the doorknob to rattle. She kept watch knowing she couldn't stay alive. Already two were gone.

Darling, darling, this world never changes. Your brothers and sisters are ghosts.

Tuesday's dead sister was named Julie. We didn't know the name of the other missing child, and we never got a call, but both Thatch and I knew another child was gone. When I pulled Julie's blue and congealed body out of her drawer Thatch said, "a regular sleeping beauty, don't you think?"

"It's definitely a suicide," the coroner said, "don't know why you had to make me come down here for this."

"How do you know?" I asked.

"Well, her wrists are slashed."

"So she's the only one who can slash her wrists?" I said.

"Come off of it, Bill," Thatch said, "obviously this guy isn't winning any coroner-of-the-year awards, but who would kill a girl like this? Probably didn't have an enemy in the world."

"You don't need enemies," I said, "just predators."

I turned back to the coroner. "I'm not going to let this rest," I said.

"She's going to rest whether you want her to or not," the coroner said.

"Julie wanted to be married under the dogwood tree," I said.

"What are you talking about?" Thatch said.

"That's what Tuesday told me. Julie wanted to be married under the dogwood tree. Why would a girl kill herself if she was going to be married? It doesn't make any sense."

"I don't know, Bill, you know that family out there is crazy," Thatch said.

"Yes," I said.

I looked over at the coroner.

"What are you wearing?" I asked.

He wore a necklace consisting of three interlocking rings.

"It's a symbol of the Triple Goddess," he said, reaching up to touch the necklace. "My wife was still a

Jehovah supporter, even after he died, but I made her throw away all of our crucifixes."

I looked back at Julie. Her face shone in sick fluorescence, the congealed blood black against her cut wrists.

On the way out of the building Thatch's cell phone rang. He answered.

"It's for you," he said. He held the phone out to me.

"Another one of my sisters is missing," the person on the phone said.

"Who is this?" I asked.

"It's Tuesday," she said.

"How did you get Thatch's number?"

"Can you come over?" Tuesday asked. "Momma won't mind. The boyfriend went out last night and got drunk, so he's hung-over now, passed out on the couch."

"Tuesday—"

"—Bill. Please come over," she said. "I don't know what to do anymore."

"I tell you what, Bill," Thatch said when I handed him back his phone, "you fuck that girl and you're going to hell."

"Everyone's gone mad," I said.

"The Triple Goddess said madness has gone down thirty percent since Jehovah died."

"Was this a double-blind study?" I asked. "Who funded this study?"

"I think the temple of the Triple Goddess funded it," Thatch said.

"Of course," I said, "so it's biased."

"Well, yeah," Thatch said, "but maybe people have

something to hope for now, you know what I mean."

"Have you converted?" I asked.

"Hell no," he said. "You know I'm an atheist."

I had a dinner of ramen and headed out to Mimi's trailer alone. By the time I got there, the night dark settled down in a haze and Tuesday stood in the driveway waiting for me.

"I'm going to die soon," she told me when I got out of my car, "now that he knows I know what happened to Julie."

"Who are you talking about?" I asked.

She smiled.

"Why did you want me to come?" I asked.

"I can't be alone anymore," she said.

"You're not alone," I said, "You have Mimi, and all your brothers and sisters."

"I'm still alone," she said.

I said nothing. The lights were on inside the trailer and I heard the children playing inside, with Mimi screaming, "Keep it down, goddamn it, or I'll smack you kids to sleep!"

"We shouldn't be doing this," I said to Tuesday.

She slipped her hand into mine. "We're not doing anything," she said. "I want to show you something."

She took me around the back of the trailer. I saw the prophet's house across the field, past the darkened deadwood and gray atmosphere like ash. His lights were on.

"Do you know who that is?" I asked.

"Yeah," she said, "he's lived there all my life. His name is Gregory. He used to be Momma's boyfriend. Before the one she has now."

"Did you like him?" I asked.

She turned toward me, walking backwards as she led me through the field.

"No, not really," she said.

"Do you like any of your Momma's boyfriends?"

"No," she said, "not really."

I stopped walking.

"Don't stop. Why did you stop?" she asked.

"I'm not really sure why I'm here," I said.

"But you came, that's all that matters."

I let her lead me to the mouth of sickened trees, their branches heavy with parasitic mistletoe, crushed under the weight of smoke and black and feral green.

"I used to go in there when I was a kid, she said, indicating the mouth of the trees, "and I'd hide. I'd pretend I was a fairy and I hid."

"You're still a kid."

"But now I'm scared to go in there. Isn't that funny? You're supposed to get less scared when you get older, not more. I wonder why I'm so scared."

I said nothing.

"Are you going to marry me, Bill?" she asked.

"No," I said, "no, I can't."

In the dark, Tuesday had no face. Her gray skin ran down her collarbone, her flavor cold, her animal eyes fixated on a point far beyond me. For every world there is a lower world. Beyond her world of Mimi's trailer and bruises beneath the hips there existed a fairy world in these asphyxiated, hollow nested trees.

"Julie was going to get married. Then she died," Tuesday said.

"I know, you told me. Did Julie kill herself?" I asked.

"No, but you already knew that."

I said nothing.

"What do I have if I don't have you?" she asked.

"The Triple Goddess, I guess. Or God, if he hadn't died," I said.

"You won't marry me because I'm not a virgin," she said.

"No, that's not it," I said.

"Then why not?"

"Because I don't know you."

"That's not so strange," she said, "I've never known anyone before."

The coyotes began to howl. We shrank. The deadwood rose up like ribcages, like the dead fields where my father used to drag horse corpses to rot and return to the earth. Sometimes death happens, he said to me once. Death always happens.

A shot rang out.

I grabbed Tuesday's hand and we ran out away from the copse, toward Mimi's trailer, jumping over wet fennel and thick weeds and death death death, the color flash of her dress. Another shot. Mimi's back porch lights came on and we appeared in the light, flushed and wild-eyed. Mimi came busting through the door in her blue flannel nightgown with a .12 gauge at her hip. The children peered out from behind her with dripping fists and red arms.

"Tuesday," Mimi said, "you hear that shot? What the hell is going on out here? What you doing out here, girl?"

"Momma," she said.

"Terribly sorry about this, Mimi," I said.

"Officer Redding, is that you?" Mimi asked.

The coyotes stopped howling. The grass rustled behind us. I grabbed Tuesday by the shoulders and whirled her around in front of me to try to protect her. Mimi raised her gun. I ducked down, caving my body around her.

The prophet of the Triple Goddess came through the grass into the light, squinting, sweat on his glass-fish skin, his shotgun raised above his head.

"What the fuck are you doing out here, Gregory?" Mimi said.

"I heard trespassers. They were talking outside my house. They were going to steal my Grandma's old rocking horse. That thing is probably worth five hundred dollars by now. It's a real antique."

"You're still a damn fool, Gregory; it's just Officer Redding and my girl Tuesday. They don't want to steal your Grandma's damn rocking horse."

The prophet of the Triple Goddess lowered his gun.

"Officer Redding," he said. He looked at me. "You came to my house earlier. For dinner."

"Yes," I said. I realized I was still holding onto Tuesday, my nails constricting her collarbone. I released her. She took a few steps back, toward Mimi. Mimi still pointed her gun at the prophet's chest.

"Ah," the prophet said, "hello Tuesday."

"Hello Gregory," Tuesday said.

"I suppose if there isn't going to be any issue, I better get home," I said.

"Bill," Tuesday said.

"I'm sorry," I said. "I'm just really sorry."

I left with the sweat sticking to my scalp, with the warm imprint of Tuesday's hand in mine, her kiss on my forehead like a mark of Cain.

I got back home and turned on the television and lay in bed with my head between my elbows and my nails in my scalp. They were still constantly running coverage on the new policies of the Triple Goddess on the news channels, and the Triple Goddess often appeared in persons and made speeches about how much better the world was going to be now, how much different, now that the evil demiurge Jehovah was dead.

I scratched at my forehead and scraped my skin underneath my nails and cried.

Five days later, Tuesday went missing.

"I know that girl wouldn't have gone off and killed herself," Mimi said, "she was too strong. I mean, Julie, well, she was a little fucked in the head. I caught her smoking Mary Jane once, can you believe that."

"You know these things can sneak up on you," Thatch said.

His cell phone rang.

"Hold on, I've got to take this call," he said. "Bill, you can take over from here?"

"How long has she been missing?" I asked as Thatch walked across the back of the house talking on his cell phone.

"Ever since that night I found you and her being chased outside by that crazy fucker," Mimi said.

"And you didn't call until now?" I said.

"Sometimes the kids go missing," Mimi said. "They usually turn up eventually. But Tuesday, she wouldn't be gone for this long. She's a good girl."

"How many are in the house now? Kids, I mean."

"Well," Mimi said, "about eight. Any idea what could have happened to her?"

I didn't want to say, well, the woods swallowed her. We have a new god but our faces remain the same. You cannot be protected by cold bones and cross chains when you cry in the night. Tuesday was right. Loneliness is our origin and epitaph.

"Officer Redding, she didn't run off with some boy, did she?" Mimi asked.

"No," I said, "I think she's dead."

"What are you talking about?"

I broke out into a run around the trailer and into the fields. Mimi called after me. I passed by Thatch on his cellphone. He yelled out my name as I jumped over a low, broken fence and into the grass. I ran toward the tree mouth, hung with mistletoe, gaping, and bent-fanged. I stopped. I had to get down on my hands and knees and crawl through the trees.

In Tuesday's faery hollow I found the four missing children, dead. Their limbs intertwined, their mouths and eyes socketed with spring dogwood blossoms, skin growing gray and grayer. I found Tuesday on her back with her dress pulled over her hips, her skin bruised purple around her wrists and throat and thighs. Her mouth was open. Fingers broken and nails scratched into the dirt. Her wrists slashed. Thatch found me a few minutes later with my hands in her hair.

"They're dead," I said. I choked. "They're all dead in here. Call somebody out here to get all these bodies."

I crawled out of the faery den, sick with vertigo.

"Jesus Christ," Thatch said.

Mimi walked over to the two of us, followed by some of her feral, green-eyed children. "What's going on?" she asked. "What happened to Tuesday?"

"She's dead," I said. "Somebody killed her. She's dead."

Thatch put a hand on my shoulder. "You going to be okay?" he asked.

Out across the field near the prophet's house I saw movement in my periphery. I turned my head and saw the prophet of the Triple Goddess standing on the porch, holding a ragged cat. He looked straight at me, his eyes bleary pale, then turned and went into the house.

"Hold on a minute," I told Thatch.

"Where are you going?"

"To talk to the prophet," I said. "Wait here."

I walked across the field toward his house. I pushed a lounging cat out of the way of the steps with my shoe and knocked on the door. No response.

"Gregory?" I called. "Open up, it's me, Bill Redding. You had me over for dinner one night, you remember?

The door opened. The prophet of the Triple Goddess stood heavy in the doorway. Up close I could see his eyes were bloodshot, with dark and puffy lids.

"Hey Bill," he said, "What's going on?"

"You knew Tuesday, didn't you?"

"Yeah," he said, "Yeah. I did."

"She's dead."

The prophet said nothing.

"Can I come in?" I asked.

"Oh well," the prophet said, "I think not."

My hands curled into fists. I dug my nails into my palms. I felt a sharp pain in my forehead where I'd scraped my nails against it last night.

"Explain to me why your goddess did this to that girl."

He said nothing.

"Can you do that, Gregory? Can you explain why your goddess claims she is all-powerful and yet allows girls to be murdered and their bodies hidden in faery graves? Can you explain to me why a goddess who exists inside of everything breaks the spines of our children, why she separates us from those who could truly love us so that she may gain power through our love, without loving us in return?"

Gregory trembled. He began to pray with eyes half-closed. He said, "Oh goddess, please protect your faithful servant from your enemies. Please protect me from the world, for the world hates those who love you."

"You got that right, Gregory," I said.

Thatch walked up the steps. "Bill," he said, "what the hell are you doing?"

"Just having a chat with the prophet of the Triple Goddess here," I said.

"Come on, Bill," Thatch said, "these murders. This is big. This is real big. We're going to get the state police out here to investigate."

"I'll be seeing you again, Gregory," I said. The prophet said nothing and closed and locked the door. I turned around and walked with Thatch out back to the field.

They got the state police down there soon enough. They dragged the bodies out while the feral green-eyed children watched and Mimi smoked cigarette after cigarette and the boyfriend paced around the trailer drinking a scotch and coke from a tall glass. They took pictures of the crime scene. They did tedious and expensive DNA testing to try to figure out who murdered this poor white woman's sick and small-backed children. They found the prophet of the Triple Goddess' spit in their mouths and his fingerprints on their wrists and throats. Big scandal. Thatch said he knew that man was a crazy, but everyone knew that.

Mimi said she knew it too, because he used to handcuff

her to the bed and choke her during sex when they were living together.

"Don't be dumb, Mimi," the boyfriend said, "plenty of people do that and they aren't serial killers."

"What do you think of all this?" Thatch asked me.

"She knew she was going to die," I said, "and there wasn't anything any one of us could have done. There's been an insidious force in this universe from the beginning, trying to keep us apart from each other."

"Maybe you should go home and rest for a while there, Bill," Thatch said.

"No," I said, "I've rested enough."

When the police went into arrest the prophet they found him kneeling on the floor in his kitchen, praying underneath his breath. When they hauled him up and put him into handcuffs, then led him away, he started to scream, "The goddess will deliver me! The goddess will deliver me!" all the way out to the police cruiser.

A limousine pulled up at Mimi's trailer. The Triple Goddess came out of the car, her bodies wearing Chanel perfume and hip-tight black.

"Well, I'll be damned," Mimi said.

We were all standing outside of the trailer in ninety-five degree heat, Mimi, Thatch, the boyfriend, the police, the Triple Goddess, the prophet in handcuffs, and me.

"So he wasn't lying," I said, "he really was their prophet."

One of the bodies turned toward me through the crowd. Her eyes were gray. She wavered in the heat.

"Yes," she said to me, "this is an unfortunate incident."

"But you're a goddess," I said. "Shouldn't you have known this would have happened?"

The three bodies of the Triple Goddess rose like arches above the crowd in their tall heels, their veins hard like shock rods against their necks and hands.

"Unless you knew he was a murderer, and you just didn't care," I said, "unless you knew and you did nothing."

"We value all human life," the Triple Goddess said.

"If you valued life, you wouldn't have let your prophet live and Tuesday die. See him in the back of that car there? He's still praying for his protection. He wants to be saved so he can continue to kill children."

"This was an unfortunate accident," she repeated.

"You didn't know, then? Then you're not omniscient, like you claim to be," I said, "you're just like Jehovah. You really know nothing about humanity at all."

"Bill," Thatch said. He put his hand on my shoulder. All three bodies turned to look at me now. The crowd silenced.

"You're not even benevolent, are you?" I asked. "You don't value human life, not really, only insomuch as it benefits you. Your powers are limited. Your powers are no powers at all. You're not even a god."

"Bill," Thatch said again, "come off it."

"That's the secret, isn't it?" I said. "Jehovah wasn't a god and neither are you. You're just the same kind of thing in a different body, whatever you are."

The Triple Goddess said nothing. The police cruiser holding the prophet backed out into the road and drove off. The crowd began to disperse. Mimi and the children and the boyfriend went back into the trailer. The Triple Goddess climbed back into the limousine and the limousine drove off. Eventually the state police left as well, so that it was just Thatch and I standing out there in the red dirt with the sun scrawled heavy on our backs.

"I'm sorry, Bill," he said, "sometimes things just happen this way."

"There never was a god, was there?" I asked. "Not one that cared for us, that wanted to cure our loneliness."

"I don't know," he said. "None of us know that. After they found Jehovah dead off the coast we thought well, here's the fake god, and then She stepped forward and well, here's the real god, but-"

"-But it doesn't work like that," I said, "it's never as simple as that."

"I suppose not," Thatch said. "You want to go back to the station now?"

"No," I said, "no. I'll catch up to you later."

Thatch left. I stood there for a while out in the front, back poised like a knife. I walked away from Mimi's house toward the field.

And I'd learned as I stood outside in that gray field with Tuesday, looking into the stretch-limbed abyss of the faery world, that the Triple Goddess was wrong.

I crawled into Tuesday's faery hole and lay down in the hollow impression her body made. I pulled at the roots with my fists, scratched and scratched over her scared nails, this once-warm body hiked up to the hips, bled out, skull scuffed, silenced by the arm and ribs of the prophet of the true living Triple Goddess. The serial killer of the benevolent. The death of a girl who wanted to be married underneath the dogwood tree, but instead had the blossoms pushed into her mouth and spilled into her collapsed eyes.

I curled into her and she was cold.

Sunshine, Sunshine

"I've been waiting for you," he said. "In these corridors you're an angel."

Mom and Dad were stiff as crinoline. My sisters were paper eggshells, Russian dolls that never took off their layers. We existed in separate worlds that only touched occasionally, such as when Mimi told me I looked like a butterfly standing out there on the edge of the garden, hesitant and shy and unwilling to spread beautiful, beautiful wings, or when Dad took me out hunting once and he let me look at the diluted universe through the crosshairs of his rifle. He shot a fox inside that universe with a little, invisible iron ball that tore its neck apart. I broke out in a run toward the fox as Dad called toward me to stop. I fell to my knees and tried to keep it breathing and stop that gaping wound from bleeding as the fox snapped and growled. It choked on arterial blood and died between my sticky red fingers. Dad carried me home in my ruined gray pinafore. The fox bit my hand, a curve of a bite like half a coffee ring – Dad had to put its mangled body in plastic and take it to the vet to test for rabies.

He never took me hunting again.

My three sisters agreed I was the wild one, like Mimi was the bookish muse, the poet, Jordan the one who carried feminine anger visible even clothed in pink patterned church dresses, or Angela, the twelve-year old sieve, running memories out between her fingers, those thoughts that belonged to her darker than we ever really comprehended. And if I was not a butterfly, I was a monkey clinging to the dark-rooted Louisiana god trees in the swamp, chasing away the fear of alligator eyes, messengers in green, but always on the lookout for the sunshine man.

Angela told the story to me. The sunshine man lived in a dilapidated, two-story house hidden in the swamp. You would know the house by its blackness like faux-Halloween face paint, windows blacked out furiously like children's scribbles, wooden slats rotting, roof sagging, the whole thing either about to collapse or burst. The sunshine man resembled his house in the way that old people resemble their pets, dressed in a black coat, boots, a velvety fedora hat, the kind of man who if he opened his coat you expected to find either blades or bats.

"Why is he called the sunshine man?" I asked.

"It's like why they call it Greenland when it's covered in ice," Angela said, "It doesn't have to make sense."

She told me the sunshine man walked the swamps at night; searching for women so he could bury his hands into their hair, make love to them not with skin but with needles and blood finger-painting, transform them with wounds and later dissect them upon his tables. He collected these women like butterflies beautifully pressed between pins, and his sunshine house hid a labyrinthine cellar maze underneath full of freezers and tubes and monsters that lived in family portraits. He killed delicately, spread out bones and skin like wings, preserving them in ice and serum, stored inside locker rooms that he visited sometimes like favorite poems, counting off delicate, torn paper haloes. Freckles and indigo eyes were his favorite lines, and he gently touched the places he drained of blood, sensual but not exactly sexual, like the smell that lingers after rain.

"You're just trying to scare me," I said, but after that I always watched out for the sunshine man. He visited my dreams, faceless as a shadow, always wearing his fedora hat and an old-fashioned coat with heavy, brass buttons. He let me touch them. Afterwards he kissed me and broke my spine.

And the four of us grew older in our separate universes and barely let our feet touch the ground. Mimi still called me butterfly even when I became awkward and chunky in adolescence, when I stopped climbing trees and started to hang out with my boyfriend after school so we could smoke cigarettes behind abandoned gas pumps and spray paint our names in visceral red underneath bridges. I learned most people might as well be faceless shadows, that forgetting is sometimes more healthy than learning, that sex felt nothing like rain. When I turned eighteen I broke up with my boyfriend, said goodbye to my parents, my sisters, and took off to Texas in a broken down jalopy that barely made it across the border. I got a job as a waitress in a diner that would have been best suited to an appearance on daytime television than in real life. I met an older man so shy he had to write 'Will you go out with me?' on a napkin after he finished his coffee and sausage. He wasn't beautiful, but he was charming in a subdued way, and four years after our first date we married in a rundown local chapel. He wore his father's suit eaten away by moths, and I saved for months to buy a yellowing, vintage wedding dress – after I tucked it away in its box in a dresser drawer I had nightmares of it decaying, decaying, decaying, the lace turning black, roach-like insects crawling over the collar.

And though I never admitted it, I still dreamed of him, the sunshine man, holding up the moon and stars between candy spoons, smiling without quite smiling, whispering seductive things.

We divorced after seven years. He packed a suitcase of clothes and left in the middle of the night, leaving me alone to ruminate through the ashes without a phoenix to rise up and claim me, or perhaps, devour me. I picked up smoking again. I remembered that old boyfriend once telling me, "You must have been an injun in a past life. What you trying to do, see gods in the smoke?" I went through so many packs of Marlboro I thought I would drown. Mimi's butterfly girl grew thin and sick and eventually forgot she had wings. I stopped making house payments. My house went up for foreclosure.

I lay in an empty living room floor, contemplating just how many pockmarked dots there were on the ceiling, when I got a call from Jordan.

Angela was dead.

In an hour I packed a few clothes, got in my car, and went back to the Louisiana swamp I had not visited in nearly fifteen years.

A funeral is much like a wedding in its frosted extravagance. Even in the presence of death we were so many parasites feeding off the silver cakes and white lilies and each other. Jordan and Mimi wore blue dresses, an awkward juxtaposition to my large and ill-fitting black suit. They were thinner and smaller than I remembered, their kisses like sandpaper, their ghostly touches reaching right through me. We said little. None of us cried. Crying would pull us out of our separate universes, our barriers, and allow us to crash and burn on another's shore like dying stars or sirens drying to the bone.

"What happened?" I asked Mom. She hadn't changed. Forever a luminous faery, a numinous scar.

"Cancer," she said. And I thought, it's always cancer, that black and white animal disease.

"It couldn't be helped, Butterfly," Mimi said.

I watched the funeral procession like a voyeur. Angela was dressed in white, her face thin and waxy, her lips red like too-ripe cherries. I was afraid to afraid to touch her as I passed by her body. I couldn't speak because all the words I wanted to say were hollowed out of me after years and years and years by separation, deadbeat boyfriends, divorce, disappointment. We were all hollow here, walking dead. We sharpened our teeth on the backs of our knuckles, fought each other like insects, and consumed skin that would never satisfy us. I knew if I opened Angela's mouth and pulled out her secret universe it would dissolve like a sugar ribbon in my hand. All of this amounted to nothing if we were all alone.

Halfway through the funeral I excused myself to go to the restroom and never came back.

I went to the swamp.

The Louisiana god trees never looked taller as they hung in the early morning mists with dormant birds in their branches. I remembered the paths I used to walk like the ache people sometimes get in broken bones that have long since healed. That's what this swamp was – a deep ache, and as I walked little pieces of me, memories, skin tissue, faery dust, peeled away until nothing remained. I found my skin hanging on a tree branch waiting for me, a little child's skin marked the wild one, dressed up in a bloody pinafore. I took it down carefully and put it on, then kept on walking until the vines were so thick in the center of the forest they roped off the light from the sun. A cool calmness descended. I lay down in the moss underneath the tree behemoths, protected from sunshine, and waited for him.

His footsteps were softer than I imagined.

"Where have you been?" I asked.

He spoke. "I've been here."

"I didn't think you were real."

"No," he said, "You did."

He knelt over me, his breath cool, his face a shadow underneath his black fedora hat. When he opened his mouth into a rictus it expanded wide, a black gap full of frozen teeth. I slipped under darkness like ether. He bent low and breathed into my ear.

"I've been waiting for you," I said.

"I know."

"Is it like when they call it Greenland when it's covered in ice?"

"What do you mean?" he asked.

I couldn't see his eyes. "Why they call you the sunshine man. Is it like that?"

"No," he said, "It's really nothing like that at all."

He bit into my neck with his razorfish teeth and I clung to him, desperate, puerile, just like the bloody girl that once clung to a dying fox because for just a moment she saw death's gray trajectory and the gray loneliness like death that lived inside her. I spilled out on the sunshine man's shoes and drank him close. The gods I never found were in his hair, clinging to the inside of his hat, gods like smoke, gods of somewhere else than this gray world.

After I was dead he took me in his arms and away from the swamp, down stairwells that reached the gutted out bottom of the world, past lockers of frozen women pinned up like butterflies. Their bones glittered in blue and red and monarch melanin scales and their eyes filled with dry crystal sugar. He laid me on an operating table in the dark. The only light came from the one he unraveled from my organs, a dully glowing bezoar, and I watched as he slit his skin apart with a fingernail and tucked it inside his ribcage cavity.

He found my wings I thought lost. He reached underneath me and spread them out from my shoulder blades, tattered and cold on the operating table, pressed my skin against needles until it stopped hurting. He turned me into a monster with his breath, his coat enveloping my face, his touch sterile, dry, clean, nothing like smoke in velvet blackness, the blood drying between my fingers, a crumbling tongue.

"Let me be close to someone," I said, reaching for my bezoar as it glowed inside of him, "anyone. Let me be close to you," and then once more, "I've been waiting for you."

He pressed his finger against my lips and whispered gently, "shh... I know, Butterfly," he said, "I know."

The sunshine man took my hand and I sat up and he helped me off the operating table. He pulled me into his embrace and I pressed my hand against his chest, and he was warm. I felt the pulse of that bezoar shudder against his skin. "Dance with me, Butterfly," he said. He kissed my forehead. I danced with him underneath the earth, underneath the cooling wires, warm and empty, and he gently pressed his fingers into my hair.

Pink Crane Girls

She's folded thirty cranes already, the coffee not even cool enough to drink. Her hands moved too fast for me to see, so that she seemed to meld into her environment, her flesh the color of the paper, her hair the texture of the brown booth. No matter how many times I saw a girl sitting across from me in that dirty roadside Cafe the speed of her fingers, the vibration of her throat and eyes, made me want to stick my head out the window and scream to the dirt.

"This is your last job, and then you're out," I told her, resisting the urge to swallow, and I thought, maybe she'll believe me,

The waitress approached, and the girl's elbow jerked across the table. Cranes spilled onto the floor. The waitress rolled her eyes, kicking a crane out of the way with her soft shoes.

"What it'll be, junebugs?" she asked.

"Hashbrowns and an order of tomato slices. And more coffee please."

"And her?"

"W-water," she said.

"And shall I call the ambulance now or after she's shot up again in my bathroom?"

"She's not on drugs, K," I said. "Not anymore. It's you know, residual effects."

"And this place used to not be a waystation for whatever sick shit you're into," she said, and then turned to the girl. "I'm not talking about you, honeycake, I'm sure you're just a good girl in a bad situation."

Before the waitress walked off, the girl had folded ten more cranes.

"This job is at the Edgar Vault. They've been waiting for us, so they've got anti-shift tech, on the walls and floors. But you're our best girl. We know you can handle it."

I used to know their names. I thought that'd make me a good manager, to show that I cared, but then I stopped caring.

She breathed in little panting gasps, sweat the color of sepia in the dawn light breaking out on her forehead.

"Sweetie."

My hand hovered over her vibrating fingers, but I didn't touch.

"I know you can handle it."

They never believed me.

***

The Lab bought up the contracts of girls who slipped through the city of fortresses, girls who slept on ceilings and dismantled machine guns for entertainment. They were girls with iron in their teeth, salt and blood underneath the fingernails. They were the kind of girls who programmed AI to go to school for them in the gridiron machine, and shot up sticky black ICE in the bathrooms of business Overlords before stealing computer codes and escaping out back windows.

Girls who knew, before The Lab even worked on them, how to get in and out. How to run. And quick.

Then the doctors took them underneath the city to our compound, put them under anesthesia, and replaced their organs and skin and bones with molecularly restructured, synthetically grown parts.

After that they always ran hot, about 110 degrees hot, and their fingers never stopped twitching.

***

Dr. Enslein, the scientist who discovered human molecular fluidity, once said the vibration of the girls was like music made of human bones, the shift his final composition, his swan song if you will, the apex to a lifetime of scientific achievement.

In his speech at the Science Symphony Gala, he didn't mention that an ill-timed panic attack could cause the girls' hearts to burst.

***

My husband once picked up strays off the street, he bandaged their paws and fed them and found them homes. I remembered playing Annihilation 6, about to take another fortified castle, when a greyhound, her nose mottled and burnt, nudged my arm.

"Get it away from me!" I said. "I don't want it here."

All at once I felt nauseated, by the wet smell of the dog, by its fur bristling against my shoulder, by its wagging tail and warm breath. It was a dog like a pustule.

"Don't you have a heart?" my husband asked me.

I didn't know. Maybe I did once. All I know is that I couldn't stand the smell of his dogs and then I couldn't stand him kissing me at night with a new heaviness, his arms wrapped around my chest with a new tension. And he said I kissed like a mirror, no curves, a barrier where my tongue should've been.

In that city of fortresses, I've learned to distrust the sun.

When we kissed I thought of the girl. The girl named White, the first one, coming through the compound doors with bandages around her wrists and throat, her feet barely touching the floor. She unraveled her hair from her forehead, in between her fingers like fireglass, disintegrating before she stopped unclenching her fingers.

I thought of her arm, half in and half out of the stone blockade in the armory, and at the sight of her limbs turning into molecular smoke her shock wide enough to break open outer space.

***

My husband said, "When I was younger, I didn't think it would be like this"

"Would be like what?"

White bit off chunks of her fingers. She was the first.

Couldn't keep them out of her mouth. She smiled a nervous smile, fingernail in her teeth.

"Leaving," he said.

"Where do they go when the work is finished?"

The bones of his favorite dog tucked underneath his arm, his favorite bottle of Cognac underneath the other. Someone like him never survived a night outside the walls. He didn't have to go a day without being fed by the refrigerator drone, or clothed by his closet style sampler program. But it wouldn't have mattered because *Her eyes were piercing sky and when she asked for a glass of water the water burst like shards of glass inside her mouth and "I'll never drink again."*

"What did you suppose it would be like?" I asked, my arm dangling off the couch, cigarette lazy piping smoke on the walls like he always complained.

"Like a bomb going off, I suppose," he said. "Like we'd be throwing furniture at each other, screaming and crying."

She asked me if we could fix this, put her back, because she could see the frequency behind the frequency. Her eyes were next-level fluids, heavy enough to crack open the space between her pupils and her mouth. She could see the wall beyond the wall beyond the wall and please, would someone put her back? Nobody should be this way.

I raised the cigarette to my lips.

"I can throw something if you'd like," I said.

"You don't have to keep being so cruel," he said. "It's over."

I thought of the wet twist pop of her bones when she expired.
It's over.

Only when he was gone did I think of where it went

wrong. I thought of the nights of being newlyweds when I sat playing virtual chess against an opponent I couldn't beat, and he stood in the kitchen in front of the open refrigerator, screaming into the icebox. I forced my heartbeat to not respond to his voice. I remembered love like being hungry. I remembered love like the back roads behind the city the government paved over to build more compounds for rich people, the roads I could no longer get to.

I said the job, hustling girls who could've been me, made me turn cold.

"We hired you because you've got the kind of face those girls can trust, but we can tell by your eyes they shouldn't dare."

But there'd have to have been a reason I took the job in the first place, knowing that I'd have to sit across the table from those shaking girls and repeat, over and over again, "This is your last job, and then you're out."

I know you can handle it.

***

Several days later, I sat in the break room with one of the surveillance crew, a thin, scratch-mouthed woman named Aiden.

"So what happened to that girl at the site?" I asked. "The one who went to the Edgar Vault?"

"You're asking questions that certain people would think require a psychological evaluation,"

"You know me," I said, picking at my Waldorf salad, "I'm as psychologically sound as the flat surface of a shallow pool. I mean, look at me. No emotional damage whatsoever. Top mental condition."

Aiden glanced at the security camera above the vending machine. A reflex, nothing more, we figured out about a year ago they weren't hooked up to anything when Jeremiah got drunk at the company Christmas party and decided to climb onto a restroom stall and unhook one after he fucked Ellenore without thinking twice.

Aiden sighed.

"You're about to tell me something fucked up, aren't you?" I said.

Her throat tightened, like she was trying to breathe without breathing, as if her lungs might explode with use underneath her overworked, stretched skin. She leaned forward, her wiry hair falling into her eyes.

"So we got her INTO the vault. She shifted through the ceiling and landed into the dome chamber like we thought she would, it was fine. But when she reached the bridge and it came time to get the codes, she-"

Dr. Brandon walked in, and Aiden's sentence hung sharp and unfinished.

"You two look guilty," Dr. Brandon said, heading toward the coffee machine.

"Aiden's cheating on her husband. It's all very scandalous. Don't tell anyone."

"Uh-huh. Is this the Filipino?"

"He's from Singapore," Aiden said, rolling her eyes when Dr. Brandon's back was turned. "And I don't love him anymore."

"Hence the cheating," Dr. Brandon said, retrieving his cup of coffee before turning back to me. "I heard that was a common reaction when unhappy people are unwilling to do the work required to improve their overall quality of life."

Before Aiden could respond, Dr. Brandon addressed me:

"Gene, do you even look at your calendar anymore? They want you in meeting room B in ten."

"Yeah, yeah, I'll be there soon."

Dr. Brandon left.

When I glanced down at my salad, I thought for a moment I saw pink paper cranes, fingertips bloodied and wrecked.

The flat surface of a shallow pool indeed.

"What happened?" I asked.

"What?" Aiden said.

"To the girl," I whispered. "What happened to the girl?"

"I mean, you know, sometimes things like this just happen. You can't always account for when exactly they're going to—"

"—What happened to her, Aiden?"

A whisper like a fierce stab.

"Aiden?"

"She exploded," Aiden said, staring at the space behind my head, not meeting my eyes. "She painted the walls. From the inside out."

***

"I keep telling myself these stories so I can sleep at night. I keep telling myself, that my pain is an accumulation of progress, that one day it will all be worth it, that the totality of who I am is being created for a singular moment of gratification. And maybe, just maybe, if I make myself blind in the right way I can construct a narrative that will validate these thoughts."

But then I see her hands, her bloodied hands, the cranes at her feet, the burning hair. I see the trail of ash she left behind her, dragging her feet across the broken tiles.

And she asks me:

"Where do they go when the work is finished?"

***

On the way to Meeting Room B, I made a detour to the girls' living quarters. Maybe the employees weren't being monitored, but surveillance cameras were positioned in every girls' room, including the bathrooms.

Some sick fuck decorated their living quarters like a Victorian dollhouse, with pink wallpaper and plush, oversized couches made of flame retardant resin and tea complete with doilies made out of steel. My brain would have shrunk in a place like that. Maybe that was the point.

Two girls sat in the common room, slumped in chairs, barefoot with toes curled hard, watching television and folding cranes. Pink cranes spilled out from their seats.

Another girl slept in the dormitory with the lavender sheets squeezed between her fists, a pool of sweat accumulating in the space next to her pillow and cheek.

"Nightmares increased by 40%," said Dr. Brandon. "Also you're supposed to be in the meeting room by now."

"You measure that?"

"Nightmares? Yeah. It's a fairly accurate barometer of one's emotional state. The content of the dream doesn't matter, but the emotions do."

I used to know their names.

I used to know their names, and I used to visit them

inside their dormitories in between assignment briefing and evaluations and one-on-ones. Learn their dreams.

"Any idea why they've increased?" I asked.

I used to wipe away the blood leaking from behind their eyes.

"No idea, really." Dr. Brandon said. "But you know, their reports you filed last quarter were rather sparse."

"You know how it is," I said. "They don't talk much."

"Is that so?"

"You don't believe me."

"I've read your reports from a few years back. The girls seemed more talkative back then."

The girl in her bed squeezed the sheets until her knuckles turned blue, and I thought the blood might rise into her throat, burst through her sweating cheeks.

"Check the logs, I can guarantee you're the only person who's read those reports in the last six months." I said. "Nobody gives a fuck about those girls."

"So that's your excuse, then?" he asked.

His face, placid as ever.

"Excuse? What excuse?" I asked.

"Someone did give a fuck. Of course they did," he said. "It was you."

***

Before my ex-husband took up housing stray dogs, he used to go to the bowling alley, with his shiny red custom-made bowling ball, his name, ANTONY R., emblazoned where the curve of his thumb rested. He sized up his six pairs of bowling shoes in the entryway and refused to store them, insisting the closet didn't know how to match them correctly.

And before he went bowling, he sat at the kitchen table for hours making macramé belts and braided rope curtains.

"Macramé comes from the Arabic word 'migramah,'" he said, "It means fringe."

I can't think of the memory of him without thinking of the frantic way he said 'migramah', of his hands scrabbling across the table, of the day when he put the macramé in a box and started trying to brew his own beer. I think the dogs came after that.

And I can't think of him and the dogs without thinking of accepting that job, and how signing the contract felt like cutting my arm off, even though at the time I didn't know why.

I know it's a logical fallacy, but sometimes I think if I didn't take this job then I would've loved him more. I could've unwound time and pressed my hands against his closed eyelids and the fluttering of his eyelashes against my fingertips would've felt like a butterfly waking up, like the maw of the terrible insect relaxing around my heart. And I would have let him in.

I would've stopped sinking into the couch, a pool of grime at my feet.

***

In meeting room B, my boss. Harris Freeman, sat in the corner of the room with his mantis-like feet propped up on the table, an ice-cube in between his teeth, cup of cold espresso balanced on one thigh.

Dr. Brandon entered the room and closed the door, shutting us into dim, windowless light.

"This is the meeting?" I asked.

"The dossier," Harris said, "On the girl we sent up to the Edgar Vault. Have you read it?"

"The files haven't been unlocked for me."

"But you heard what happened to her," he said.

"No sir."

He rolled his eyes. The cup, balanced precariously, wobbled, and espresso spilled out onto his jeans.

"Of course you have, Gene. I know you've got ears."

I sighed, and sat down.

"She…." I trailed off.

"Exploded?" Harris asked me.

I nodded.

"Yes," Harris said. "Gene, let me ask you a question. How long has it been?"

"Four years, two months, and two days, but who's counting." I said. "Why?"

"No, I didn't mean the job."

Dr. Brandon leaned against the door instead of sitting down. A slice of light cast down from the halogen bulb above his head, making it appear like he was some kind of sick, and pale deliverance angel.

"I mean, how long has it been since you've left your, I'm sure sterile and uninviting dark apartment and socialized?"

"I don't see what my personal life has to do with any of this."

"You been to the arcade lately? Spun through a halogen storm? Gone to any cocktail parties? Met a gentle, but well cultured man who's recently going through a divorce? Called your mother?"

I said nothing.

My boss checked his phone.

"Maybe you're into the dark stuff. Maybe you got divorced because of your insatiable sadistic impulses. You know there are all sorts of simulators in the V district. Have you tried any of those?"

"I'm not sure-" I said, but he interrupted me.

"-Or maybe you can take a hike to the mountains. Enjoy a new kind of solitude. You know, if there are any mountains left. Have you checked? Are there any mountains left? Have we drained the ocean yet?"

"What is this meeting about again?" I asked. "I'm not sure I'm clear on that."

He checked his phone again.

"We've locked your computer and your code access. Gene, it's been a pleasure working with you. A security guard outside will see you out."

"This is a joke," I said.

"No," he said, and he grabbed the espresso cup, brought it to his lips. "I wish."

"On what grounds am I being fired?"

"Fired?" my boss asked, looking at me over the rim of his coffee cup. I'd never noticed before, there were little flowers painted on the edge of the cup. It appeared they reached up to brush his eyes.

"It's an ancient art, Gene. Ceramic pottery was found 18,000 years ago in the Yuchanyan Cave in southern China."

I'd forgotten, my husband also got into pottery. I'm pretty sure that was before the dogs, but after the macrame. The image of his fingers, encased in clay, spun into my head. Then just as quickly-

"No, Gene. You're not being fired. Just think of it as an extended mandatory break."

"Is this because of the girl?" I asked.

"Everything," Dr. Brandon said, "is about the girls."

"You think I had something to do with this? With her... accident? I didn't. I stuck to the script. Like I always do."

"You're making this difficult for yourself," my boss said. "It's just a job. All you've got to do is walk out the door. The security guard will escort you out. Turn right. Go get a cup of coffee from the cafe. Take a fucking break. We'll call you."

"They're all unstable. The molecular structure folds. I'm not a scientist. How can you possibly blame me?"

"Take. A. Fucking. Break," my boss said.

Dr. Brandon touched the desk beside my hand. I almost felt the pulse in his wrists, throbbing mad, the rest of his body like a sheet of ice, struggling to contain something bubbling underneath the surface.

His mouth twitched, as if he was going to speak, but he said nothing.

I stood up and without a word, headed toward the door.

"If you get a chance, go to the south side and eat a vanilla macaroon on the digital sunlight balustrade," my boss said to me as I left. "They say it's just a fad and that real sunlight will be in again soon, but I think it's better than the real thing."

***

40% increased nightmares.

That first girl I managed, White, acquired her contract

after she was imprisoned for hacking into the mall's infrastructure and replaced all the advertisement audio with an audio book version of Finnegan's Wake.

I never knew her real name; it was a protective measure in case I was to be questioned. So she was always White to me, because of those synthetic, glowing braids she wore that hung down to her waist. For weeks I dreamed of her shifting through the walls of banks and estates, those white braids whipping forward with the force of her movement, dripping with acid, spraying the ceiling and floors until they ate away and collapsed the entire building. I dreamed of falling through floors and floors with her, down elevator shafts and through mazes of scaffolding.

I took her to that roadside Cafe, away from the sharp buzz and white perspicacity of the lab. I used to think taking them out to lunch before I told them where they'd be ripping out their spines and bleeding their colors made me seem, somewhat human.

"This is your last job, and then you're out," I told her, like I told all the others.

But unlike the others, I remembered her favorite color was pink, just like the cranes she folded, and she used to have a boyfriend named Siph who broke up with her because she put a key logger on his computer. She had a cat named Geoffrey and her favorite book was, strangely, War and Peace.

And when she dreamed, she dreamed like me, of falling and falling and falling.

Dr. Brandon told me the dreams would go away soon, once I got used to the job, and they did. Mine would, at least.

40% increased nightmares, and here mine had stopped. But maybe for the wrong reasons.

"Go on sweetheart," I said to her, picking her burnt fingernails off the floor. "You can do it."

Girls like her didn't cry, not often, but her tears were like cigarette ash, burning and black. And the day I learned she'd gone on her last job, heart pulled out of her throat as she shifted back through the walls after opening the front doors for a rush job, I picked up my keycard, walked out of the building, went home, and sobbed.

My husband put his arms around me and said, "Maybe you should quit. The stress is too much."

"We know what's going to happen to us, you know, even if they don't tell us," White said to me, eyes like burning static.

"Gene?"

Her death didn't make me want to run, it made me want to return to The Lab and pick up the fingernails of another girl off the floor. I wanted to press back the bleeding heart with my palms on her chest. Even if I stopped caring, the price of being that close to blood, I could still do that.

***

I sat in the simulated sunlight cafe, eating a vanilla macaroon and watching a scarlet ibis dip its beak into the fronds in a glass-like pool. On the way to the cafe, Aiden called me.

"I heard you got fired," she said.

"I didn't get fired."

"We've got to figure out what's going on. I play poker Friday nights with one of the administrators. I could unlock your file and get you into the building-"

"Now you sound like the one who needs a psychological evaluation," I said.

I suppose I should've felt the upheaval of leaving the building, without warning or explanation, after all those years of employment. Not knowing when I'd return should've been a violent thing, like a Gordian knot dripping with stomach acid, an angry pulse in the center where it couldn't get out.

But I only felt stillness, like for the first time in a long time the storm brewing in my head, making my thoughts incomprehensible and dark, was cleared.

"Yeah," Aiden said, and she sighed. "It's a silly idea. I just don't know what's going on."

"Your job is safe," I said. "Don't worry."

I entered the cafe, the sunlight brushing the backs of my hands, I ordered a latte and the aforementioned vanilla macaroon, phone cradled to my ear, and sat near the pond in the back. In the late afternoon, the cafe was nearly empty, enough for me to hear the sounds of humming insects through the walls.

"You still there?" I asked Aiden.

"Yeah, I'm thinking. It's just, we've been working together for so long."

I said nothing.

"Hey, it wasn't your fault. The girl," she said.

"Maybe not," I wrote. "But there are plenty of things that are."

Another pause.

If I looked into the space beyond the projection of simulated sunlight, into that dark dense space between the wall and the sensors, I started seeing ghosts made out of sparks. Ghosts that existed only in the in between, between a grounded object and one pushed outward.

"You remember what happened with Dr. Enslein?" Aiden asked.

***

"Why the cranes?" I asked Dr. Enslein, while he was signing my copy of THE MELDED GENIUS on his international book tour.

"Excuse me?" he asked.

"The cranes," I said. "Why are the girls taught to fold cranes?"

"Are you with the press?" he asked.

"No sir," I said.

Behind him a girl sat, her back to the line going out the door, her pink dress unzipped and revealing the layout of her protruding spine. It didn't seem like a real body part, but something holographic, simulated, a real spine wouldn't be on a girl constantly humming and vibrating to frequencies we couldn't comprehend.

Dr. Enslein wouldn't tell the audience that when a girl was molecularly structured, they had about 7 or 8 shifts before death, before the entire infrastructure collapsed and her heart and knees and brain gave out.

"I know about the rapid firing in the basal ganglia," I said. "The Blepharospasm that affects the eyes, the increased neurological decay. I understand before the cranes, the girls would often break their fingers or bite off the tips because of the speeding up of the nervous system. But why pink cranes?

"Who do you work for?" he asked.

Behind me a group of young graduate students, wearing thick-rimmed glasses and blazers too expensive for actual scientists, jostled me.

"I'm not at liberty to say, sir," I said. "I work for a private firm."

He sighed, obviously debating whether he should call security to have me removed and potentially slow down the line even more. But, he chose to speak.

"We knew we had to keep the girls occupied, and in such a way that was uniform and easily taught, but complex enough so that their minds could focus," he said. "And my daughter. Well, she loved origami."

The girl, her lips like a trapped hummingbird, leaned over and whispered something in Dr. Einslein's ear.

"She wants to talk to you," Dr. Enslein said.

"About what?"

"Come around the table, you're holding up the line."

One of the graduate students let out an exasperated sigh. I slipped around the table and headed toward the girl. The air around her was hothouse warm. I knelt beside her, my knees crushing a crane.

"I heard," she whispered. "Y-you work with people like me."

"Yes I do," I said.

"You're good at what you do."

"I don't know," I said. "I'm going through a divorce."

The skin around her eyes shone with bruises from the rapid fluttering of her eyelashes.

I didn't know why I told her that, why it slipped out of my mouth so easily, when I'd been holding onto it tight for months, trapped between my throat. Like she reached through me, faster than I could perceive, and grabbed it with no resistance.

"M-maybe I-I'll see you again," she said. "And then y-you can tell me you're doing good."

A finished crane dropped from her fingers. She glanced up at the line, at Dr. Enslein, who was bent over signing another copy of THE MELDED GENIUS. Then her body lurched forward, and she broke apart.

It was like watching a person transform into living color, her fingernails into trails of sand, her hair into an empty gorge. Her skin melted away, revealing the smears of her her blood and ribs and spine, for less than a second hovering in space, before they too dissolved.

She rushed forward.

In less than a second, she reassembled in the center of the crowded auditorium, the force of her arrival pushing people out of her circumference. Dr. Enslein stood up, knocking a stack of books over.

"Anna!"

I swear, she looked back at me. Like an insect, she looked back, without moving anything except her neck. And she couldn't smile, not with the humming composition of her face, but it was almost as if she wanted to.

Then she looked up, and shot through the ceiling.

Dr. Enslein shouted for security. People caught in her path patted their bodies up and down, as if to make sure she hadn't ripped out pieces of them on her way through. Others began crying or heading for the exists. A few seconds later, the fire alarms went off.

I slipped out the performer's exit before anyone could

question me about what happened. I left the building and walked through an alleyway through the dark, heading toward the streets under groaning, titanium walls, between lights like bullets coming through club windows. And I found myself looking up at the sky, beyond the steel wiring, which I never did anymore. The sight of those mile long buildings shooting into space, as if the curvature of the earth would be sliced apart by their piercing height, always made me feel as if I was shrinking.

But I was looking for her. Of perhaps, whatever remained of her, glittering scraps of bones and skin. And I thought of White, long dead by that point, her fingertips exploding into supernovas.

"Where do they go when the work is finished?"

Maybe pieces of all of them were up there in between the fortresses of the city. Maybe when they burst apart, their heads and tongues and brains, their molecules kept shifting, over and over and over, in and out of darkened vaults and computer banks. Never able to be caught.

A small comfort for a manager of living time bombs, for the one who attempts to ease the transition into a melting death.

My phone rang. It was my soon to be ex-husband, now living in temporary housing about a mile north.

He often called in those days to ask if I'd seen one of his knick knacks - the Peruvian rug, the stuffed raccoon paw, the blue clay vase he broke in four pieces. He spoke in this quavering, desperate way - a child lost in the dark warehouse of his toys.

I imagined answering the phone.

"I could've sworn I left those soap antlers in the closet," he'd said.

And I'd pause, trying to refrain from saying. "Stop calling me. You don't care about any of these things and I certainly don't either. You will not find answers in clinging to dust-covered, useless relics you collected searching for the thing that is you."

Trying to refrain from saying, "Find someone to fuck so you'll stop calling me."

Imagining, after taking a deep breath.

After looking up and imagining supernovas of skin and glittering, superspeed ropes of nerves.

After a silent wish on an airplane I mistook for a star.

Saying:

"I don't know where your fucking antlers are. I don't want to bury myself in quiet distractions but you'll always be consumed with searching for them. One day things are going to change at The Lab, and I want to be there."

Yeah, I know, I'm probably going to forget this moment ever happened, with the girl and the sky and the instantaneous epiphany that what I'm doing means something. And as the months drag on I'm going to even more apathetic and cynical and hopeless. But maybe one day when a girl explodes, I'll be able to pick up the pieces and put them back together. That seems worth the cost. That seems worth losing some of my humanity."

And after a pause, he'd respond:

"I've taken up leather tanning. Did you know the tanning process is written about in Homer's Iliad?"

I couldn't help it. I leaned against a nearby building, dizzy and nauseous. I turned my phone off, and I smiled.

***

Alone at that roadside cafe, I could breathe. I thought it must've been something in the air, the cloying dirt sticking to the inside of my lungs. The Lab psychologists told us it was "Beneficial to the girl's well being" to occasionally show them clear skies, roads free of dark metal and disco light. I always wondered why they thought this unfiltered air was beneficial to anyone.

But it wasn't the air that was the problem - it was the constricting of my chest.

A man walked in with a girl, and they sat down at an adjacent booth. The girl's skin vibrated, her fingernails chipped, fingers like the music of a theremin. They spoke in low tones, the girl nodding, nodding, folding, folding.

The man got up to go to the restroom. I glanced sideways at the girl, who waited for that moment to sob. She stopped folding the cranes, pushing them out of the way with her elbow to give herself the room to collapse face first into the table.

"Hey," I said, my voice soft.

She didn't respond.

"Hey," I said a bit louder. "I know you're from The Lab. I know what they want you to do."

She glanced at me, her tears boiling on her face. Looked at me like a question.

"I just want you to know, there's another way."

And I pointed up.

Out of the Slip Planet

When I first came to the black island I visited with a young man named Powderkeg. When I spoke his name he clicked his teeth and rocked back on his heels like he'd been hit with a shotgun. He lived on the cove and drew dirty portraits of his wife in the black sand.

"The ocean took her from me," he told me, hunched over in the sand and tracing thick lines for his wife's mermaid tail. "The ocean here takes everything."

Powderkeg never went to the town meetings to sit in the animal face chairs and discuss politics with the elders who had necks like paper cranes and scaredy crow hands. Powderkeg called them suckers, those elders with cancerous white spots in their mouths who passed a peace pipe around a circle and inhaled amnesia. He said they only remembered where they had been, and not where they were. He said men were not welcome on the black island, that we all should have been born rolling thunderclouds.

Powderkeg and I watched the tide bring in another dead porpoise. This one was lean and silver gilled, with a spot on his nose like an oil patch. The sand stuck to its skin and dried into a translucent, crusty second skin.

"Shouldn't we do something?" I asked. "Can't we save it?"

"What you want to do?" Powderkeg asked. "Push the poor bastard back into the ocean so he can go beach himself on another stretch of shore? Trust me, it's better this way."

Powderkeg chewed on a piece of cinnamon like a cheroot. It crumbled into pieces on his lap that he never bothered to brush away. When he came by the house, I knew better than to offer him a cigarette or a drink. The first time we met, I asked him if he wanted a shot of whiskey. His eyes grew real wide, like he'd just been shot in the stomach.

"Are you the devil?" he asked me.

"No," I said, "my name's Hector."

He laughed then, a choked laugh full of spit.

"Okay, Hector," Powderkeg said, "I'm not doing any of that stuff anymore. No drugs, no women. The ocean ain't going to take me again."

The porpoise died while Powderkeg and I sat watching on the porch. Night descended on the beach and the moon rose above the waters, its jaw ringed with a cannibalizing red. Powderkeg stood up and pulled a packet out of his back pocket.

"It's time," he said.

"Time for what?"

He opened the packet and tilted it out in his hand. Flower seeds spilled into his palm.

"I'm a guerilla gardener," he said. "I'm maximizing my positive karma intake."

"Guerilla gardener?"

"I sneak into people's backyards and plant flowers without them knowing it."

"What?"

"Can all you do is ask questions?" Powderkeg said. "Don't answer that. And guerilla gardening requires more finesse than you think. Want to come with me?"

"There's something I have to do."

Powderkeg left without another word. I went into the house, poured myself a shot of whiskey, and went into the attic. My workshop waited underneath the dark-tinted, ocean-mouthed window, its belly heaving against the floor and sides scraping the walls. Laid off to one side was a row of gleaming tools, delicate bird-headed incisors and scissors shaped like gray dog legs.

In the center of the table was my latest project, the ostrich egg-shell. Yesterday I removed the egg yolk with a syringe, cleaned the egg shell with warm soap and water, painted its surface in transparent glaze until it shone.

I picked up my tools. I began carving away at the pattern I knew would soon emerge from the white, like a sentinel that appears out of a snow storm. Then when I was finished, it would join its brothers and sisters on the mantel above the worktable, next to the picture of my daughter.

Nobody else knew about the egg carving until the day girl, Serafina, came into my house one day like an elastic band, bouncing from wall to wall, gravity disappearing underneath her feet. Her pale blonde hair shot up to the ceiling like a tornado. She brought me cupcakes in a plastic container, just like her Grandmother made them, vanilla sugar with pink frosting.

"I won't see a man who doesn't have ambition," Serafina told me. "Do you have ambition?"

I didn't want to lose the only woman I knew on the black island, so I led her to the attic and showed her the mantel where the carved eggs lay like an exhibit of discarded uteruses. She sucked in her breath and stood still when she saw the mantel, so that the tornado of her hair lay flat against her shoulders and her arms became pale and quiet. I took her in my arms and licked the pink frosting off her lips.

"Oh, they're so pretty," she said, "but what do they mean?"

Serafina didn't really need an answer. All day girls are looking for love girls. She led me into my bedroom. She lay down on my bed with her eyes rolling back in her head and told me to take off her dress. I knelt down and slipped the dress over her lamb thighs, the soft splay of blue veins against her bikini line like fireworks. She wore pink underwear the color of her grandmother's frosting.

"Can I be your muse?" she asked me when we were finished, when we lay splayed out on the bed touching each other's naked bodies like children. "When you're working, will you think of me?"

"I'll try," I told her.

But as I worked on carving the ostrich egg, I could only think of the dead porpoise that beached up on the shore, encrusted with black sand. I tried to concentrate on carving the egg shell with the delicate bird mouthed incisors, trying to envision the shape and structure beneath the soft white. I needed my head to be white, but there was only the black.

I looked out the window and the whipping froth of the ocean rolled up and clamped its jaws on the dead porpoise, dragging the corpse down into the waters below. When I looked back at the ostrich egg I didn't see the pattern I'd designed, but the face of my daughter.

I crushed the egg with my fist and swept it off the desk. Sixteen discarded and crushed eggs lay in a basket underneath the desk. Each one bore the face of my daughter.

The ostrich eggs were expensive, luxury goods I received from a foreign dealer in the mail, special order. I'd ruined the last of the shipment, and would have to wait until more arrived to begin work again.

The attic walls throbbed like meat, like the angry pulse beating in my neck. I threw my instruments down on the ground, knocked over my lamp, paints, syringe and brushes. I stood panting with everything strewn about the attic floor. I looked at the picture of my daughter and I tore at my hair and the tufts of my regrowing beard.

It was a school picture, the kind of photograph that's airbrushed until the cheeks shine like celestial powder and the hair radiates like a halo. In the picture she wore her nervous smile, the smile that makes me feel hollowed out inside. My daughter had panic disorder - anxiety attacks that left her hauling her dark hair against the floor like a ocean that rose up to swallow her whole. She couldn't talk to strangers. That school picture smile was broken, the smile of a victim baring her teeth.

Not the smile I used to know when my daughter and I took our walks along the shore in the night, the cool shadow that kept her hidden from the world. The comfortable smile of a girl in her secret universe.

But I only had left this photograph with the panic smile, and that universe of her had disappeared for me forever.

Someone knocked on the door.

"What do you want?" I called out, thinking it was Powderkeg back from his guerilla gardening.

A few seconds later, another knock. When I answered the door I found a dark haired woman leaning against my porch balustrade, her legs like vipers, skin the color of honey. She wore a velvet robe that was stitched with a map of the stars, tied at her waist with a sash. Tanya, the night girl.

"Your friend was in my backyard again," she said.

"He's planting flowers."

"Idiot," she said. "Nothing grows here anymore."

"Are you sure?" I asked. "I thought I saw something grow once."

"Come outside," she said.

Tanya liked to make love on the hammock tied to two poles beside the ocean, in the place where the tide ran in and spilled underneath our bared feet. When we got to the hammock she untied her robe and draped it over the hammock like a blanket. She was naked underneath, honey colored except for the fevered white scars on her wrists and waist. She told me her former husband held her captive in their basement for six years. He tied her up with barbed wire.

"'You may hate me, but you'll never forget me,' that's what he said," Tanya said once. "'Think what you want of me, but I won't be forgotten.'"

I lay down beside Tanya in the hammock and I kissed her sunspotted cheeks. She didn't return my kisses like she usually did, but stared off into the sky until her eyes glazed over like there was a plate of glass keeping her from me.

"What's on your mind?" I asked.

"They're bulldozing my house to put in a new road,"

Tanya said. "The elders in the town meeting discussed it last week."

"Is there anything you can do?"

"I can appeal, but they won't listen to me," Tanya said. "And I won't be able to afford another house. I can't get a job. The world stopped needing me a long time ago."

I kissed the knuckles of her hand, then the white scars of her wrist. She spoke as if she was addressing the ocean.

"It's stupid, getting attached to things, but I love that house. I loved going out on the balcony in the morning and smoking my cigarettes, sitting in the office while I write and the moon soaked my hand like it's healing me. That house has all my scars. And now I'm going to lose it. Just because some crusty old people decided they needed a road to go straight through it."

I wanted to say that I was sorry, that she could live with me, that I would give her money, a loan, but I could only think of my daughter and her victim's smile, the crushed eggshells sitting underneath my work desk.

"Maybe you could appeal for me. They would listen to you," Tanya said.

"Why would they listen to me?"

"You're not from around here, they know they can't just push you around. The rest of us, they know we're going to die here no matter what so they don't give a damn."

"I'll think about it."

"Please, Hector," she said, "go to their next meeting and appeal for me. They'll laugh me out of the room but not you."

"What are you two doing?" someone asked.

Powderkeg appeared in the dark like a floating smile.

"Are you being naughty again?" he asked, then laughed. "That'll get you so many negative karma points. You'll be stuck here forever."

Tanya, not bothering to cover herself, stretched in the hammock so that all her sinews gleamed taut.

"Why are you always hanging out with common whores?" Powderkeg asked me.

"Go away," Tanya said.

"I'm just warning my friend. If you cared about him at all then you wouldn't do this to him."

"I know you hate me," Tanya said, "But it isn't my fault nobody likes you and you'll be alone forever."

When I looked at Powderkeg he stood straight, shivering. The curve of the moon struck him sideways, seemed to bend him down into a flat space.

"Hector likes me," Powderkeg said, his voice quiet.

Powderkeg slipped away.

Tanya and I had sex as the tide rushed in and out with our breathing, and when we were done we lay for a long time without speaking, touching each other's soft spots, our hair. I drifted to sleep.

I dreamed of my daughter.

I dreamed of her crib, which she once said she could remember as the bars of an iron cage. She started crying so I picked her up and rocked her, whispered hush. My daughter kept crying. The walls of the nursery flaked away like gray skin. My daughter kept crying.

"Hush, hush dear," I said, and anxiety swelled in my chest, in my fingers that held up her head, as if it were seeping from her into me. My wife's shadow, weakened with osteoporosis, hunched over wheezing in the corridor.

Powderkeg crouched on the windowsill, while he tipped packets of seeds out onto the floor, one by one.

I rocked her until my nerves turned into quicklime. She kept crying. The walls of the nursery tore away and the stars rushed into my skin. Powderkeg was sucked out into space. My wife's shadow blew away and gravity crushed me down into an unceasing black hole.

I awoke on the hammock, alone, with my daughter's cries echoing over the waves.

I got slowly out of the hammock. The black tide came in, and then receded. At first I thought the flapping, bulbous shapes left on the beach were mermaids. The moon struck them in crazy light, shooting slivers of black and white down their backs that gleamed and twisted and snapped. I stepped backward and tripped over the hammock, and fell down in the sand. Only then did I realize they weren't monsters, but a school of porpoises.

They made trembling noises like kittens, their mouths opening and closing. Sand encrusted their silverfish teeth and gray skin. The moon barreled down into their blowholes, which were raw as exposed tumors.

I wanted to save them. I wanted to get up and run out to greet them like a war hero, press my shoulders into their sides and push them back out into the ocean. Except I imagined once I touched them their bottlenecks would become aquiline noses, their seaweed entangled throats would turn into wet hair. I would touch gray skin and it would become pink and cool. They would turn over on their backs and look at me with dying woman eyes that had seen leviathans, shipwrecked vessels, the blue heart of coral reefs.

I got up and went back into the house. I locked the doors and pulled down the window blinds, then poured myself a glass of whiskey. I went up into the attic and sat on the desk with my legs crossed, spine bent down like a drinking flower, and I recited the Hindu mantra my daughter's therapist once gave her so she could get through the night:

Asato mā sad gamaya

From ignorance, lead me to truth

Tamaso mā jyotir gamaya

From darkness, lead me to light

Mrtyormā amrtam gamaya

From death, lead me to immortality

The next morning I went to the town hall to talk to the elders. The town hall on the black island used to be a bar, and when I walked up to the steps and pushed past the gray velour curtains over the door the first thing I saw was the dead neon beer bottle sign still nailed to the wall. At first I thought the town hall was empty, it was so dark and muted inside, but as I stood there someone whispered in my ear, her voice like a machete at a rabbit's throat:

"Close the curtains."

The curtains fell back into place. As my eyes adjusted to the darkness I saw the elders, sitting on animal backed chairs, their coats made out of serpent smoke, black masks of pig velvet.

"What business do you have with us?" one of the elders asked.

I pressed my hands to my throat, but I couldn't feel my arteries beating blood. I seemed to be full of smoke. Something about that room made me spin out of my body, nauseated with the fog.

"Well? We don't have all day."

"Tanya," I managed to say, swallowing with difficulty. "I'm here for Tanya. Her house is being destroyed to make a new road. She doesn't have anywhere else to go."

"Tanya," the woman with the machete voice said.

There were no windows in the ancient bar, only silver grills and voodoo masks. I put my hand on the wall to steady myself, and ended up sticking it into a stuffed lion's mouth.

My daughter could not survive in a place like this. Better for her to curl up into the crook of an ostrich egg than be folded up into the smoke of the town hall.

"Can you do anything for her?" I asked.

Silence.

A thought: I've been here before.

Then laughter. All around me, cooked up slowly, laughter like someone turning on a garbage disposal. I pressed my fingers into my temples and tried to see where the laughter was coming from, but it was all around me, inside of me.

"She doesn't have anywhere to go," I repeated, but by then it was too late.

The laughter kicked me in the stomach and I found myself running out through the curtain and back outside.

It was night outside and the streets were empty, all the shops closed. The moon stained purple the water pooling in the ditch. As I walked away the blood rushed back into my body and I took gulps of air, clear and clean, and I learned to breathe again.

I thought of the porpoises washed up on the beach.

When I got back home I found both Tanya and Serafina on my porch.

Tanya leaned up against the balustrade smoking a cigarillo, wrapped in her robe of stars. Serafina lay reclined on my rocking chair like she was on the deck of a cruise ship, wearing a bright pink slip and having one leg draped over a rocking chair arm. When I approached they both looked up at me, their eyes streaked wet, pupils large as black horses.

"Where have you been?" Tanya asked me. "We've been waiting for you for hours."

"You both always look too picturesque to be real," I said, my voice distant, "how do you do that?"

"Cut it out," Tanya said. "Have you been drinking?"

"No," I said.

"Serafina, go pour him a drink."

Serafina rose from the rocking chair. The moon slapped her pink dress and she curved, shimmering, like a beam of light. Tanya beckoned for me to sit down in the now empty rocking chair.

"I'm sorry. I tried to talk to the elders about your house. They wouldn't listen to me."

"What happened?"

"They laughed at me."

When Tanya leaned back her robe of stars fell open at the waist, revealing her fevered white scars.

Serafina came back outside and handed me a glass of whiskey.

"Powderkeg's gone insane," she said.

I took a drink. Swallowed.

"Isn't he already insane?" I asked.

"No," Tanya said, "we don't mean planting flowers in other people's backyards insane."

"He's going to kill himself," Serafina said, "he says he's figured out it's impossible to get anymore karma. Or something. I don't know. I never understand what he's saying. Will you go talk to him?"

"You want me to talk to him," I said.

Tanya and Serafina said nothing. I set my drink down on the porch.

"Where is he?" I asked.

Tanya pointed up toward the cliffs and her map of stars grew into bones that lifted her up and tilted her throat back.

I found Powderkeg at the top of the cliffs overlooking the ocean. He wore a beige bomber jacket, and sat on an enormous, woman-haired rock, facing away from me and out toward the ocean.

"Powderkeg?"

He lifted up a jar and a red can of kerosene and set it down on the rock in front of him. .

"Powderkeg?"

He poured kerosene into the jar, glistening amber, and raised it to his lips. I ran toward him and tried to knock it out of his hands, but he downed the entire jar in one gulp. Swallowed.

"Oh, Hector, there you are," he said.

"Tanya and Serafina said you've gone crazy," I said.

"Tanya would say that about me," Powderkeg said, "Bitch."

I crawled up on the rock beside him. I grabbed the red can of kerosene and hurled it out into the ocean. Then I grabbed the jar and smashed it onto the rocks. Powderkeg slumped over on the rocks with his arms in front of him, limp as wax, a thin line of kerosene oozing between his parted lips.

"Why'd you do that?" he asked.

"You're sitting up on the cliffs drinking kerosene. Don't ask me why I did that."

"Don't you know the rules don't apply anymore?" he said.

"What?"

"At first I thought I could've changed things," Powderkeg said, "I thought if I reversed this karmic process I could have saved us all. Not the porpoises, I don't care about them. But you. Tanya. Serafina. Your wife. Your daughter."

"Wait. What? My daughter?"

Powderkeg trembled. His face was hard as nerve-wire. His limbs ticked like bombs.

"Do you even know where she is anymore?"

I said nothing.

"It's because she's gone. Or, well, it's more like you and I, we're gone. As far as she knows, we don't exist anymore. I mean, we exist all right, I just don't want to believe it."

"Powderkeg, let's get you home."

Powderkeg started to choke. He vomited and spattered the rocks below with kerosene.

"Or the hospital, maybe."

I put my hand on his shoulder. He laughed. Wiped his mouth with the back of his hand.

"Listen to me, you might not ever get a chance to understand again," Powderkeg said, "You and me and Tanya and Serafina and the others - we're going to keep spiraling downward and nobody will be able to catch us. Karma, baby."

"Karma?"

"Is that all you can do? Repeat what I've said? Yes, karma. Cosmic justice. Whatever you want to call it. When you die, if you've been bad, you go to a place just a little worse off than where you used to be. But what happens when the process can't be reversed? When the world you've been placed into denies you a way to escape?"

"You're insane," I said.

"There's always a lower deep, didn't you know? However bad you think it can get, it can get worse. And Hector, it's going to get really bad."

He coughed again. The back of his trembling hand shone with vomit.

"Look," Powderkeg said, and he pointed out toward the beach near my house, "the porpoises are coming in."

I looked down below and I saw the ocean bringing in a dark mass. The creatures that beached up onto the shore were naked, white skinned, hair like gray foam.

"Those aren't porpoises," I said.

"I know," he said.

Powderkeg laughed. I jumped off the rock and ran down the cliff toward the beach, where the dead women waited on the beach. They were sprayed with salt, twisted bones, so anorexic that their rib cages jutted out and played music with the moon. Their eyes were still open, with a thick, glaucoma sheen. I knelt into the sand and lifted one of their heads into my lap, the hair gently choking me.

"Powderkeg!" I called out.

No reply.

When I looked back I saw the rock he sat on only moments before, now empty.

"Serafina! Tanya! Someone help!"

I looked back toward my house and saw only the abandoned porch, the rocking chair scraping along the bottom of the rotting wood

I almost wanted the dead woman in my lap to turn into my wife. My daughter. Anyone that I knew. But she remained faceless, a stranger.

I released her and ran toward the town. The moon kicked up sand and followed me, slicing at my heels. I reached Tanya's house and found a construction crew in blue uniforms surrounding the property with a bulldozer and weapons of destruction.

"What are you doing?" I asked one of the men, a giant, baby-faced monstrosity with skin so translucent I could almost see his arteries pumping.

"We're tearing this house down," he said.

"In the middle of the night?" I asked. "Where's Tanya?"

"She doesn't live her anymore," he said.

I went to Serafina's apartment in town. The door blew open.

"Serafina?" I called out.

I went into the kitchen. On the counter were undecorated cupcakes just out of the oven, with the pink frosting waiting in a ceramic bowl beside them. I went into the bedroom. The walls were painted with blue and green hibiscus flowers, the bed clean and made.

But she was nowhere to be seen.

I left her apartment with my blood sinking. The wind whipped up a froth, and a storm came in from the ocean. The moon, drained pale, rocked back and forth like a hypnotist's coin. I pressed my face into my coat to try to protect myself from the cold.

"You should be getting inside," someone said to me in a familiar, machete voice.

The elder woman from the town hall stood in front of me. She was thin and stunted, with black nails three inches long and eyes of powdered glaze. She wore a white bird mask, and molting feathers stuck to her neck and forehead.

"Where did everyone go?" I asked. "Where's Powderkeg? Tanya? Serafina?"

She opened her mouth, but instead of responding a stream of smoke spilled from between her lips. Then she turned and walked off.

"Son of a bitch! Don't you walk away from me!"

She turned the corner and I followed after her. She walked through the curtains of the town hall and disappeared.

I ran after her. I pushed open the curtains of the town hall with such force that I fell onto the floor. I sensed the elders all around me, bones rattling, sloughing off their snake skin, drinking malt liquor and smoking black cigars with their folded back, boneless fingers.

"What have you done with my friends?" I asked.

The room exploded in laughter. I pressed my hands into my ears and hunkered down on the floor, knees and elbows against the tile. I thought for a moment I'd slipped into my daughter's skin. So this was what it felt like to be an anxious wreck: every time someone looks at you, a hammerhead shark slams you in the ribs, every time. And to think I never knew.

The laughter flushed my cheeks and scorched my brain. I lifted my head and started screaming.

"Stop! Stop it! Stop!"

And just as soon as the laughter came, it stopped.

I rose to my feet, shaking. I choked on the heavy air and stumbled toward the bar. I grasped a bar stool to try to gain my balance, and swiveled around on my feet to look back at the elders sitting in the corners of the room.

"I'm too tired for this. Tell me now," I said. "What have you done with my friends?"

"Powderkeg?" one of the elders asked, his voice the voice of a toad.

"Yes. Powderkeg. Where did he go?"

"He's not coming back."

"Why?" I asked. "What have you done with him? Before he disappeared he was talking some nonsense about karma, or cosmic justice, and how - maybe we were put here because we've been bad?"

"Nobody put you here. You came here because the laws of the universe cannot be reversed."

"What?" I said, "you're kidding me, right?"

I laughed. Nobody moved.

"The cosmic wheel determines your position in the universe after death. Those who have accumulated negative karmic points will be placed on a lower planet, as ordained by the law."

"If we keep going to worse and worse places, than we can never escape, can we? Like Powderkeg said, there's always a lower deep. We're not created in vacuums. We're shaped by the circumstances around us. How do you expect someone to be a saint in hell? That's absurd."

"It is not absurd. That is the law, and it cannot be altered."

"So what happens then? Worse and worse worlds just keep being created? You have people like Powderkeg trying to secretly plant flowers in people's backyards? And how does he know about this anyways? Have you been telling him this nonsense? Are you the ones who gave him that kerosene to drink?"

Nobody spoke. In one the corner the woman with the bird's mask shifted in her seat, and when she lifted her head I saw her neck was flecked with gray, reptilian scales.

"Is that what happened to my daughter? My wife? They just disappeared one day?"

No reply.

"And what about me? What's going to happen?"

"Probably the same."

"But why?

I stepped away from the bar stool and tried to steady myself on my own feet. I swayed, unable to gain my balance. The equilibrium had shifted from underneath me. Gravity spun around my head. Took a nose-dive into the bar counter.

"Why?" I asked once more.

"Addictions to mood-altering substances. Sexual intercourse outside of marriage. Transgressive art. The failure to keep your wife and daughter intact. You've been attributed many negative karmic points. Your next reincarnation will be in a lower planet.

"Who came up with this shit?"

No response.

"Don't answer that. That doesn't matter. I didn't come here to get a lecture on this nonsense," I said, "tell me where my friends are now."

"The ocean took them."

I laughed clear and firm, but I didn't believe it for a moment.

"I'm done with this," I said. "This is some trick you're all playing on me, isn't it?"

I left the town hall much the same way I did the first time, with smoke running through my veins and my eyes floating to the top of my head. The cool night air cut into me, and the buildings were the only things that emerged out of the earth. Nothing living grew here. I'd known, but it never seemed to matter before. Until now.

I wondered if the black island took away my daughter's courage. If nothing, not even the Hindu mantra, could've saved her because we were in the lower deep, and the universe would have never let her escape. Maybe she and her mother were always meant to disappear.

I arrived home. The dead women on the beach were gone, if they were ever real, leaving nothing but black sand and the hammock on its poles, deflated like empty skin. I pressed my hand to my chest and felt my heart swinging, swinging, ready to smash into my ribs and crush me.

A package waited for me on the porch. Ostrich eggs. I picked up the box, gently, and I took it inside my house. Inside the house I placed the box on the coffee table and opened the box. Inside the eggs, like mottled carbon, waited in individual, foam-padded nests.

I left the eggs on the table and sat on the floor, in front of the couch, lotus style. The moon outside peered in my window like a horse's eye. The ocean screeched and for one long moment, I thought the elders might have been speaking the truth. Maybe the ocean took my friends, took Powderkeg, Tanya and Serafina. Took my daughter and wife and the dead women too. Took the anemic porpoises and Powderkeg's cinnamon cheroot. One day it would open its mouth, teeth made of coral rose, and swallow the city underneath.

Perhaps we had all arrived on the black island from somewhere else, after death, and when we died again we would go somewhere else worse. A lower deep.

I closed my eyes. I listened to my breath, and my heart slowed. I recited the Hindu mantra.

Asato mā sad gamaya

From ignorance, lead me to truth

Tamaso mā jyotir gamaya

From darkness, lead me to light

"Oh, fuck it," I said before I finished.

I threw the box of ostrich eggs on the floor and crushed the eggs with my foot. I went into the kitchen to pour myself a glass of whiskey. I walked out onto the porch to wait for the ocean, black and boiling, to bring my friends back with the tide.

Honeycomb Heads

One night The Residents carried our children away while we slept. We searched for them on the frozen surface of the planet with our satellite and snowmobiles. We found no traces of them left on the ice, no scraps of hair or clothing, not a drop of blood squeezed from a finger, no footprints of either Resident or child. The Residents stole several of our security cameras, so we couldn't trace the direction they'd disappeared. Even our omniscient satellite remained silent about their whereabouts.

"Maybe they never even existed," said one of our childless professors.

Late at night I sent a message to Central Station near Earth: *Why the fuck did you send a philosopher with our colony?*

Of course, I never received a response.

It was our biologist Anja who found the grid-like entrances to the underground reserve where The Residents lived, camouflaged in ice and unlocked only by body heat.

Our colony governor advised we shouldn't go in. Our central satellite couldn't map the tunnels underground. There could be new species with new diseases. We could carry viruses with us back to the colony that would teach us nothing except new and unusual kinds of pain. I've been talking to the professors, and maybe our children never even existed?

Central Station overruled her and authorized investigation into the reserve.

Several of us went underground in hazard suits with supplies to last for two weeks. We travelled down a network of dark, warm tunnels. We had no directions, except down. In two days our communication devices stopped working. We lost contact with the colony. We couldn't even talk to each other behind our thick hazard suits, and communicated by turning our flashlights on and off, by tugging on each other's shoulders, pointing at our feet when it was either collapse or sleep.

In a week we reached the substrate, where walls glowed, flecked with warm, golden dust. We sweat underneath our hazard suits. My eyes burned with sweat I couldn't wipe away. Before I arrived at the colony I spent my entire life in southern California, possibly the last desert on Earth, and once went to the hospital for 2nd degree burns from the sun. And yet I couldn't even remember being this hot.

I thought of turning back, but then I thought of Tammy.

In a week and a half, weak from our liquid diets, our heads buzzing and red skin on our faces peeling away, we arrived at a long, lit hallway. Amber-liquid cells honeycombed the walls. We found our children in stasis inside of them.

They regained consciousness when we pulled them out

of the liquid, but they were sleepy and slow, barely able to move.

I found my daughter Tammy in the last cell, her dark eyes open but unseeing, her blond hair a nest for her wrists. She kicked her feet, languid little sleepwalker's kicks. I plunged my arms into her liquid cell and pulled her out. I tore the helmet off my hazard suit.

"Mommy?" I said, gasping in fetid underground air. "Can you say Mommy?"

She spit bubbles.

"Can you say Elle?" I whispered, trying to clean her wet face with my sweat-soaked shirt.

The others pulled off their helmets and stripping away their hazard suits. They shook their waking children, trying to force them to speak. One of the scientists started yelling about toxicity and viral possibilities, but it was difficult to listen to him when my daughter was coughing on my hands as I cupped her chin, as she tried to open her eyes with fluid stuck to her lashes.

She vomited amber liquid on my arms.

"Where are they?" someone asked.

"Where are the Residents?"

In the center chamber past the honeycombed hallway we found the Residents, sloughing off their chitin and dying in piles of quivering muscle. The queen sat on her throne of glittering dirt, gorged on honey, her stomach bloated, her lips glistening.

"Why did you take our children?" I wanted to ask.

I wanted to stick my hands through the warm dust brushed onto her stomach, to pull out her viscous blood and smear it across her face. I wanted to break her fingers and see if she, this creature undiscovered and under researched, light years away from earth, knew how to scream.

The seven eyes rolling in her head snapped toward us. Her mandibles clicked, echoing through the large chamber. She held an arm out toward us, stretching it so far it dislocated from her shoulder with a loud pop. Glittering blood poured from her wrist, and she died.

We travelled back through the maze. Though we abandoned our heavy hazard suits in the hallway of cells, it took us longer to get to the surface than it had to go down. We carried the emaciated children on our backs, in our arms. There legs atrophied and they could only walk a few minutes before collapsing. Their skin stuck to our skin with sweat, but they were cold.

Back home at the compound, we cleaned the crystallizing amber off the children in the showers. We wrapped them in warm towels and lay them down to sleep. As night came, the temperature-regulating shields went up. The beasts out in the dark, beasts with ice-colored fur and ridged, protruding teeth, came out of their dens and wrestled each other and hunted and wailed. The children shivered and rolled in their beds at the noise.

We were beginning to think that moving here was a mistake.

Earth had been dying for a long time, no surprise there. Overpopulation, over-pollution, war, and a failing economic system. It's a story that the Vikings were singing thousands of years ago. We poisoned the rivers and obliterated mountains because the human brain is physically incapable of understanding long-term consequences. Good thing we discovered space travel before we all went bankrupt.

Several planets had been found and colonized in the

last fifty years by private organizations searching for the promised land, some sweet milk and oil that would make them rich enough to live in private galaxies after Earth collapsed. We could've gone to Indica where the blue dust of the planet that swept across the plains was a sweet, mild hallucinogen that seeped into the pores of skin. Or we could've chosen to go to Enslia, where colonists breathed cold fresh air that smelled of flowers, and bathed in hot springs so pure that the water cured their arthritis and closed up old scars. We could've even gone to Mars, where residents lived in domes built from nanite machines and were coddled by robots. The best literature and movies came from Mars, produced from a society that never forced its people to die on factory lines or mines.

Instead we ended up on Frigg, where ice dunes ridged the surface of the planet. At night when the sun plunged down behind the polar mountains the temperature could fuse our organs together with cold.

"It's not so bad here," our architect Taylor said once. "I've heard of things going horribly wrong on other planets. Something in the habitation process, or the machinery malfunctioned. You heard what happened to the people on Deus, didn't you? Apparently the government got involved and everything. "

Taylor pointed toward the sky.

"Good thing she's kept us safe so far."

Only at night could we see our satellite, big as a moon, hovering over our planet. Its gears worked in silent space, but sometimes I thought I heard it talking to me. In my dreams I sat on top of a curved hill, freezing to death, unable to speak. Yet the satellite extracted my thoughts.

They traveled to her through space on a silver thread.

I don't trust you.

"You don't trust yourself."

What have you done with my daughter?

"You blame me?"

You could have warned us.

"Why would I?"

She rearranged the stars to smile.

"Why would I?"

The doctors administered nutritions to the children through IVs because their stomachs couldn't hold down food. The children screamed in pain as they slept. The doctors injected them with antibiotics and painkillers. They kept screaming. The children shivered and clenched their teeth as they slept throughout the day.

In the morning before the sun rose, the children awoke for an hour or two. They stretched and stirred, pressing their emaciated spines to the bed, rocking from side to side.

Throughout the barracks parents cried, "Can you say 'Mommy'? Can you say 'Daddy'?"

The children didn't speak. Their blood pooled in their veins. Their hearts beat at half speed. Before noon, they'd slipped back into sleep. This continued for a week.

A second week.

By the third week their bodies resembled pieces of gray furniture. When they opened their eyes their pupils did not shrink in light. They were dilated, broken into fractals, swirled in red. I thought they'd collapse underneath the weight of their bones.

Before all of this, I once asked Tammy where she thought her soul lived. She laughed at me. She had her father's laugh, the kind of laugh that made you want to sink down through your own skin.

"You're silly," she said. "You know it doesn't matter."

We were beginning to think they'd never fully wake. The doctors came and went every few hours. Parents stood by their child's bedsides, piling on blankets, taking off blankets, adjusting the lights, smoothing foreheads, trying not to break their own fingernails against their cheeks.

"What was it like underground?" someone asked, clutching at locks of her child's colorless hair.

"Warm."

While everyone else shivered in the cold, those who went underground were heated and red. I pressed my face against the cold barracks wall, trying to cool myself. My stomach felt ready to rupture. When I took a shower my top layer of skin cracked and peeled away.

And as our children continued to sleep, we became insomniacs. We couldn't close our eyes, because maybe our children would walk over our eyelid and disappear.

Our scientists had taken vials of the amber substance from the tunnels to study. In our lab they found the amber was a sort of prenatal fluid. The cells were like amniotic sacs, filled with proteins and carbohydrates.

We traveled millions of lightyears across the universe to get away from earth, only to find creatures with the same protein structure we possessed, molecules once spit out of a star factory that bloomed into single-celled organisms on the surface of a desert world. Life was not an anomaly. Only a bad joke.

Taking samples of the children's blood revealed their veins flowed with Resident DNA.

Anja invited me into the communal kitchen to talk. Anja used to smile in a way rare for scientists, blushing up to her eyes. On earth she'd become the department head of her research lab, yet on weekend nights still performed at the Venus Lounge, a chanteuse who dipped her skin in gold and sung forties jazz songs.

I was told she would've made Billie Holiday rip her hair out.

She hadn't sung in years. Not since she came to Frigg.

"What's happening to our children?" I asked.

"Isn't it obvious?"

Anja poured me a cup of coffee. I hadn't drank coffee since we came back from the tunnels, and looking at it made my insides squirm with heat. I set the cup down on the counter

"Let me guess, I said. "When The Residents kidnapped the children breathed the prenatal fluid, they mixed their DNA together."

"Elle, has anyone ever said you should be a scientist?" Anja said.

"This is me rolling my eyes at you."

"But that's not everything," she said.

"Do I want to know everything?"

Anja looked down, tracing her finger around the rim of her coffee cup. When she flexed her fingers, the skin on the back of her hand cracked and bled.

"No, you don't want to know." She said. "This is why I never had kids."

"Because you thought they'd be captured by aliens and their genetic code restructured? That's a stretch."

"Because I get too attached. It's a poor trait for a scientist."

"Not for a parent."

It was difficult to believe that the thinning, sleepy thing sinking into dirty sheets could be my daughter.

Tammy had her father's tousled blonde hair, his energy. Everyone used to say standing in the same room with her father was like being struck by lightning, and Tammy was no different; touching her was a static shock. She wanted to be president. A model. A writer. A veterinarian. She wanted to create a machine that would build for us a new dimension where we could hide when we wanted to be alone. Somewhere we could walk in the forests and not run into a thousand other people walking the same path.

She seemed to defy the laws of spacetime. All at once she could be jumping on the couch and running through the kitchen, breaking cups, smashing cabinets.

The camera her father gave her before he walked out on us never left her wrist. When she wasn't singing and dancing and screaming, she sat on her computer and cycled through photographs of her eyes.

"I'm trying to find myself," she said.

"I thought you said it didn't matter."

At that Tammy sighed, like I'd never understand.

Why, no matter how fast our computers ran, no matter how far we extended our fingers in space, could we not ever get back to the origin? In my eyes, I would not find myself. Forget the soul, forget God, forget essence; even if I tore open the zygote that fused to form me, I would not find myself. If I travelled to the loneliest planet in the universe and set up shelter there, deprived of all unnecessary accoutrements of society, I would not find myself. I would only find the face of a cold mountain, an underground honeycombed hive, my reflection fading in the bronze mirror of a metal lake.

I'd find my daughter, floating in a cell breathing amber fluid that'd make her forget those eyes belonged to her.

***

One night, the children woke up.

***

The children tried to leave their beds. They kicked and screamed when we held them down. I hit the alarms, and doctors rushed into the barracks. The sedatives did not calm the children. The painkillers didn't keep them from screaming loud enough so we couldn't hear each other speak.

Tammy's eyes were wild and filled with adrenaline.

"Do you remember who I am?" I asked as I held her down by her shoulders.

She said "Mommy" like being kicked by a horse. "Mommy" like the last spitting spark of output from a machine being destroyed by a virus.

The other children spoke.

"Mommy," they said, their voices blurring into each other. Mommy.

They screamed and screamed. The doctors examined their bodies searching for pain points, bruises, infections. They pried open the children's mouths and checked for swollen tonsils, red throats. They checked their hearts, beating fast but to be expected. The scientists filtered in and took more blood samples. Some of the children flushed yellow. Some started vomiting. They strapped a gangly, writhing boy to a stretcher, but not before one of his flailing arms struck a young doctor in the mouth. They wheeled him off to the lab for x-rays. The doctor stopped for a few moments, her hands over her face, her body rigid.

"He drew me flowers once," she whispered, and then fled.

"We need more straps," a parent called out.

His child pushed him, and he fell. When our children stopped eating, many of the parents did as well. How easy it was, to dissolve underneath stress. When he hit the floor he broke his bones. His child reared up from the bed. I chased after him. I caught him by his skinny arm and pulled him into my embrace. He screamed louder. Tammy jumped up from her bed. I screamed louder. She'd send a lightning bolt down on our heads. She'd tear the walls down with a sideways glance. So many weeks without movement, comatose and thinning, I thought her heart might burst.

Tammy ran toward me. An old part of my brain thought she wanted to touch me.

Instead she touched the boy convulsing in my arms. They grew still. They clasped hands and touched foreheads. She breathed cool breath into his mouth, he breathed warm back.

I released him. They nuzzled each other's necks and sank onto the floor, the color returning to their faces.

We let the children go. They rose from the beds and met in the center of the room. They interlocked hands and huddled together, thrumming, rubbing shoulders. The doctors carried off the man with the broken bones. The children huddled closer. Breathing in. Breathing out. Their screaming, now subdued, still rang in my ears.

They slept together like a Rat King, whose tails have

been matted and tied together underground in darkness, the bones fused. Several organisms, now one. I could not see Tammy in the pile of children, so tightly they held each other. The only part of her visible were the ends of her blonde hair.

Whenever anyone tried to pull them apart, they cried out as one, a throbbing, swelling insect noise. We couldn't inject lullabies into their brain stems. We couldn't cradle them to our chests and administer medicine that would teach them how to be human again.

The professor of philosophy speculated they were a new evolutionary step of the human race, but he didn't know a goddamn thing. The head of the biology department, Doctor Einsler, suspected the Resident DNA acted as a virus that would override the human parts of their brains.

"And do what?" I asked.

That, he didn't know.

Their bodies gave off a new kind of heat, their skin drenched in cooling sweat. Their eyes grew a film across them and they no longer used them to see. They saw with their fingers, grasping and studying objects they once found familiar, reaching out for each other and keening if they ever found themselves alone. Maybe they were like insects, searching each other out with pheromones buzzing on their noses and lips.

They sat outside in longs rows touching each other's backs. Tap. Tap. They relearned words with fingers encrusted in powdered snow.

Maybe "Love" meant a thumbprint of ice on the lips.

"Feed me," a brush of powder underneath the chin.

Hannah Pash, six years old, once wanted to be the first

president of Frigg. Now she stripped the skin off her fingers and dug into the ice with her toes, hissing at any adult who touched her.

Little Ben used to be obsessed with time. He drew diagrams of a clock tower he wanted to build in the center of our colony, even though we were all synced to the master clock. When his mother tried to give him his grandfather's antique watch, he smashed it on the ground and picked through the tiny gears searching for food.

They fed each other droplets of artificial honey and reconstituted packages of dried ice cream and powdered strawberry. They sucked on their fingers until they bled. They keened like coyotes as they grabbed at their growling, shrinking stomachs. What did The Residents eat? We didn't know.

Why did they steal our children in the first place, and why did we enter their inner chamber to find them in ritualistic death, their queen holding her wrist out toward us? We didn't know.

"Why don't we know?" I asked Anja.

"We didn't think we needed to," she said.

Anja went to the Doctor Einsler and requested permission to study The Residents. Not so fast, he said. There was red tape to go through, papers that needed to be signed. Requests for armed guards to accompany the expedition. Funding to be acquired. And anyways, they would send someone else. They needed her to continue study on the cross pollination of new GMOs.

"Fuck that," Anja said.

She set off on a snowmobile one morning through the temperature-regulating shields. She carried a tranquilizer gun and what rudimentary examination tools she snuck out of the lab.

At night I imagined her trying to sleep and cook dinner outside in the freezing cold. Every time a beast wailed, I imagined her being trampled underneath him. At daybreak, I climbed to the top of the barracks and searched the horizon line for her, waiting for her to return.

She didn't even have any children of her own, yet she was the only one who ever went out to search for answers.

I didn't cry like the others at first. I found parents weeping in bathroom stalls, weeping behind refrigerators. Schoolteacher Miss Madison lay curled up in my bed after the children refused to come to class anymore, a mask of blankets over her face. The doctors dragged her into the medical center where she stayed for a week.

While the children chittered and played with each other and clawed at the frozen dirt searching for a way into the earth, the parents formed a wailing wall. They hugged each other while the children interlocked arms and legs in a Gordian knot of skin. They talked of abandoning Frigg. There were planets where people could drink the dirt like rich coffee, planets where the sun healed disease.

And besides, we didn't have it so bad on earth. Sure, it was crowded. Sure, only the rich could afford oxygen masks and the rest of us had to cross our fingers that cancer didn't metastasize in our brains, but we killed all the animals that could kill us back. We never had to worry about freezing to death or being trampled by iced-back beasts. Tammy and I had our own apartment and a tiny kitchen table that we couldn't eat at without bumping elbows. We had warm food and coffee that didn't make my stomach want to crawl inside out.

I had Tammy.

I signed up for the waiting list to leave Earth before Tammy was born, and when we had the opportunity to leave I thought for once Tammy would be able to stretch her legs and not hit another human being with her feet. She could see mountains and breathe pure air. Several of her classmates were already coughing up polluted black blood, others on multiple medications for stress and anxiety and ADHD and depression and fatigue.

We came to Frigg four years ago. Central had not sent anyone else since. Communications had come infrequently and brief. Four years, and we had yet to discover resources that would churn a profit or even how to take care of ourselves. Th

The only time Tammy still let me touch her was when I brushed her hair. She sat quiet in her tiny pink chair, staring at herself in the mirror. It was the stare of meeting someone you've only known in a dream, of trying to remember.

"Tammy," I said. "That's you."

Her eyes never blinked.

I brushed her hair until it turned the color of powdered snow and fell out. I collected the hair from the floor and tied it in a ribbon, hid it in my pillowcase. It was only hair, I told myself, hair doesn't mean anything. Yet I couldn't deny the way losing her hair changed the shape of her face.

After all the children lost their hair, we started finding teeth embedded in the snow. They spit teeth out into their hands as if trying to get rid of a bad taste.

Anja still hadn't come back. Nobody suggested sending out a search party, we were too busy crying on X-ray sheets.

I couldn't cry. If I cried then the monsters would come out of the walls and the snow. If I cried, all the water would drain out of my body and I'd be a husk to be swept under the carpet, or a skin blanket for hospital patients. I'd have to cry for every terrible thing that happened to me - in chronological order - for the death of my parents from the blood-congealing cancer, for Tammy's father leaving me, for the last time I ever looked at earth on the shuttle out. How earth resembled a tiny ball in space, like a marble on black velvet, its waters poisoned and brown. How I felt skinless in that moment. Gutless. You only get one origin, and we'd ruined ours. Soon the earth would die, and we'd never get to dive down into the pools that we crawled from millennia ago.

Please, don't make me cry.

The children dug into the ice until their fingers bled.

Then, as if they'd been waiting for this tragedy, news from the colonization program came. Our colony was being dismantled. Frigg had been declared inhospitable and unprofitable, like we'd known all along. It was time to find a new home.

We didn't have to say it out loud to know. The children wouldn't be coming with us. We'd been mourning them since the night The Residents came and stole them away. The doctors stopped treating them, their parents turned away, brushing away the tears frozen on their cheeks. By the time we were ready to board the ship, they'd have mandibles where their mouths used to be.

I found Tammy in my bed with three other children. They tapped out symbols on the backs of their heads. Most of their teeth were gone. Their flushed skin cracked and peeled away. They wriggled out of their skin like The Residents in the tunnels, leaving shells of themselves behind. Underneath they were translucent, their organs dark and crystallized.

"Do you want to go home?" I asked her.

She did not blink when she reached up and removed the eyes from her head.

I grabbed her hands. Her eyes, those dark, all seeing eyes, fell onto the ground. The earth started to shake. No, it was me who was shaking. My hands seized up. My tongue curled to the back of my throat.

"Help," I whispered, but nobody heard me. The other children fled.

The lab was empty. The kitchen was empty. The dormitory was empty. Darkness fell. The temperature dropped. It had been daylight only a moment ago, hadn't it? Difficult to tell, how long I'd been on the floor searching for eyeballs. Maybe I'd lost my sight as well. Maybe the darkness was blindness, they children had infected me with their fingernails, the soft seductive hush of their hearts collapsing into dust.

Scrabbling on the floor, for the first time in years, I cried. I fell to my elbows, choking, shuddering.

My daughter climbed onto my back.

"Mommy," she said.

"Please," I said.

Though I didn't know what I begged for.

The colony was packing up, taking what they could. They were probably talking about going to Enslia, someplace with warm air, someplace where they wouldn't risk waking up in the middle of the night with their limbs turning black from frostbite.

The industrial buildings we built would degrade. The

temperature-regulating shields would use the last of the battery cells, and power down forever. The signals would go quiet.

The satellite would continue to hover over the planet, watching the empty spaces, waiting for instructions that never came. On self-regenerating cells, it would wait forever.

Mommy.

She shivered and I lay her down in bed. I kissed her forehead. I kissed her decaying mouth. She touched the spaces where her eyes used to be. I wanted to tell her, "You could have been a photographer. You could have been a ballerina." I wanted to tell her, "Life isn't fair, but this. This is beyond unfairness."

For the first time since I pulled her out of the amber fluid in the tunnels below, we slept together.

And I dreamed.

I dreamed of a tapping against my stomach, a tapping against the back of my head. It first seemed random, but then I realized there was a rhythm, like a complex piece of music. I was surrounded by children. They breathed soft against me, their eyeless faces pressed into my back and throat. Tap. Tap. Tap.

I dreamed their touches streaked rich colors against my skin. They painted geometric shapes across my mouth. This was not the mad, frenzied dance of insects. Food. Fuck. Fight. This was an ancient language, of cosmic and astral beauty. It was a language of emotions, embedded deep into the skin. Through their taps they showed me the history of the universe. Stars burst into life and exploded in death. Planets bloomed like flowers. They took me to the birth of Frigg, the ice on the surface so hard and thick it could not be penetrated.

They took me deep underneath the surface, into the reserve where The Residents lived. Their touches traced a network of tunnels, no longer a pointless maze built by mindless insects, but a neural network made of synapses rubbed off fingers, a structure made from the memories left on decomposing shed skins.

There were palaces down there built out of crystal. There were underground fields that went on for miles. Bright jewels grew on the ceilings like suns. They took me to meadows of lush grass past the amber cells. They took me into libraries of touch. Resident librarians passed their knowledge through fine fingerprints. History and physics and fiction were told through impressions of bodies.

With a touch they showed me we made a mistake.

I woke up with a start. The children surrounded me in bed, reaching out to touch me. Their eyes fell out of their head. They spit out the last of their teeth. I could hardly differentiate between them anymore. They were all soft-shelled insects, caught in collective ecdysis.

I went out into the dark. The creatures in the distance howled. It had taken years to prepare this colony, but it was as if only in preparation to leave it. I found the scientists and engineers in the ship's central station, running through the protocol of tests before takeoff. People were stowing away what little belongings they had left. They, like the children, had grown film across their eyes.

"We need to go underground." I said.

"Where the hell have you been?" Doctor Einsler asked me.

"Why did we never go further underground? All those years we searched and suffered, and we never thought to look below us?"

"There's nothing down there except the Residents and the tunnels."

"You're wrong," I said.

"How do you know?"

"The children told me."

"The project has been cancelled. We aren't getting any more funding."

"What about the children?" I asked. "What about Anja?"

"Forget about Anja. She went AWOL and knew the consequences. And the children, they're not ours anymore."

The ship rocketed out of the planet's gravity as I curled on cold ice. I was alone with the children.

They tapped on my back.

Come on.

They're waiting.

I crawled to my hands and knees and struggled to my feet. I hadn't been eating. I hadn't been sleeping. I couldn't feel my fingers or my toes. I seemed to not be in my body, but hovering above it.

Come on. They're waiting.

I took the last vehicle left behind, a rover with half a tank of gas.

Come on.

The children piled into the vehicle. My hands were so cold I could barely work the controls. The children touched my face. My spine. My body seemed to extend out past into theirs. I drove the rover past the heat regulating shields. The temperature dropped even further.

Their hands drew a map on my body with dripping honey and fingers and spit. They guided me across the ice, through herds of snarling, fighting creatures, through forests of frozen trees, dead for thousands of years. They forgot how to speak with their mouths but the language of their fingers dripped colors into my brain.

Keep going. Come on.

They're waiting.

Tammy's breath was sweet in my ear.

The gas ran out and the rover shuddered and stopped. We climbed out and walked across the frozen landscape on foot. I thought we would freeze to death, but they created a barrier for me with their tiny bodies. We were warm together. They urged me forward when my legs wanted to give out. Not much further. Not much further.

We came to an underground entrance and climbed down into the tunnels. We no longer needed hazard suits or flashlights. The way had been laid out for us in the trails of glittering dust. We touched the walls, leaving behind red streaks. The children's organs, black and crusted on the surface of the planet, glowed underground.

They were luminescent.

Underground we came to a golden field. We were warm for what seemed the first time in years. Heat flowed back into my blood. Creatures like fireflies danced in the dark. The children dug through the dirt and grass and unearthed translucent fruit.

Tammy held one out to me, cupped in the palms of her hands. I took her gift. It tasted like spiced honey.

I found Anja in the field, wrapped in white sheets, her skin dipped in gold. She no longer had a mouth. She talked to me with her fingers.

The shapes told me a story.

We can remake ourselves. We don't have to yearn for

who we used to be. Nostalgia is a lie, and this can be your home.

Deeper into the reserve, Residents were being reborn, shining, from the husks they once crawled out of.

Tammy touched my face.

My name is not Tammy, she said. My name is fingers dipping into cold dust, a warm fingerprint. Step into the amber. You too will have a new name. A beautiful name. Feel the liquid wash over you. You never knew your brain could think thoughts like this, geometric puzzles. You never knew that it could remember a history older than earth.

The amber pulled me in. It cooled my bones.

Welcome home.

The Dog that Bit Her

Every night my wife June stood with her arm outstretched over the threshold of our door, eyes closed, waiting for me to come back home and take her hand. No amount of time on a psychiatrist's couch, no medication, no reassurances could convince June to close the door and go inside before I returned.

"A neurosis born of childhood trauma and fear of abandonment," one psychiatrist said after the other. What was never taught in the Freudian hell they were spawned from was that knowing the origin of a problem rarely dispelled it. Tell me doctor, what is logic to the red-headed woman with the numb arm outstretched, shivering until her eyes almost fall into her palms like seeds? See her here, knuckled white, holding her tattered skirt together with pins, her hair blowing so hard in the wind I think it might punch the moon. Watch me disappear, cease existing, until I close my hand around hers and lead her back inside.

"One of these days something's going to snatch you away," I often said to her. I lead her over to the couch when I got home and I kissed her chin. She clung to me without speaking.

"I thought you would never get home," she said like always. "A butterfly landed on my hand, and I thought it was you. But it wasn't. It was just a butterfly."

"I'm here," I said, "I'll always be here."

As she lay beside me in bed curled around me until it became hard to breathe, I thought again of leaving her. But the next morning I prepared for work, kissed her on the forehead, and left. Only to repeat the process the next night. And the next.

But before I go any further, let me explain to you the beginning of all this. The only reason to tolerate such a restricting neurosis from a woman would be to have a neurosis of your own, wouldn't it? I can't say for sure, as I've never been one to roam the neuter-washed halls of the psychiatrist's office pulling my brain out until it stretches into a jump rope. Maybe it was because my mother taught me chivalry, or I had a savior complex. Maybe it was because, despite the ghost she'd become, that I truly loved June.

But I'd like to think it was because of the white dress.

We were both sixteen and shy and our parents arranged all of our dates because they probably thought without their intervention we'd be virgins forever. Chaperoned, like in the old days, we walked side by side without touching - gloves on our fingers. I talked until my tongue became numb. June rarely spoke. I kept trying to coax her into speaking to me, telling me something about her, anything to close the gap between her and me.

"Pretty weather today, isn't it?" I said, almost cringing at the words.

June uttered a soft "Yes," and looked at the ground.

"When I was younger I used to climb those trees over there," I said, and I pointed out toward the grove of persimmons on the horizon.

"Oh," she said.

I looked back behind me and my father was trying to look inconspicuous as he stood behind a mailbox sipping a cup of coffee. When he saw me looking at him he winked and gave me a thumbs up.

"You want to go look at the trees? Here, I'll take you."

She made a noncommittal sound and stiffened when I slipped my gloved hand into hers. We walked underneath the persimmons trees and I kept thinking that this scene should've been idyllic, perhaps even romantic, what with the orange blossoms of the persimmons and the overcast sky like a sugar rush. I'd read stories of young love and I wanted to bury my fingers in her bright red hair and kiss her gently like virgins do. But there was only the stiffened fingers in my own, the silence between us. She tensed when I brushed the beetle off her shoulder.

I told my mother I didn't want to see her anymore.

"Why?" my mother asked, almost frenetically, so that the tomatoes she was cutting up transformed into a murder scene, "What's wrong with June? She's gorgeous."

"I don't think she likes me," I said. "She never talks to me."

"Of course she likes you."

"I don't want to see her anymore," I said, and the dates stopped.

A few weeks after we stopped seeing each other, a knock

came on my bedroom window. I was in bed, reading Kafka or something equally pretentious. I thought at first the knock was the tree scraping against the pane as it always did when the weather turned fierce. But the knock came again, louder this time. Then again. I threw the book on the bed and peeled back the curtains. June stood outside my window in the crooked bower of the tree, her hands grasping at the limbs, her toes barely touching the ground like those of a ballerina mid pirouette. She wore a white weave dress, almost translucent, and I could see the dark nipples of her barely-there breasts protruding from the fabric.

I opened the window. She spoke to me, but in the wind I couldn't make out her words.

"What did you say?" I asked.

She spoke again.

"I can't hear you," I said, "come here."

I outstretched my arm for her to take. She unhinged herself from the tree and took my hand. This time we weren't wearing gloves, touching only skin on skin, and she didn't stiffen up as I helped her climb through my bedroom window. When I had closed the window to the wind, I turned back to her.

"Okay, now what was it that you said?"

"Hey," she said quietly.

She looked like she crawled out of a dream, wild girl in the white dress, bra-less and barefoot. I thought at any moment she'd detach herself from her limbs and metamorphose into a vine sticking straight out of my wall.

I moved toward my door and locked it, slowly so that the latch didn't click.

"Why are you here?" I asked.

"You stopped seeing me," she said. She looked at the ground when she spoke this, and her hair fell over her eyes.

"I thought you didn't like me."

"I like you," she said.

I sat down on the edge of the bed. I spoke softly, afraid that any moment my mother or father would knock on my door.

"I couldn't tell," I said.

"You're smart, and kind," she said, "and you have eyes like an owl that once broke his wings in my backyard and died in my arms. And when you touch me it's not like the other boys touch me. You touch me like, I don't know, like good philosophy."

I continued to sit on the edge of the bed, unable to move. I opened my mouth to speak, but it was as if it was stuffed with leaves - I couldn't speak. This was the most I'd ever heard June say.

When she took my head in her hands her fingers shook as if I was an electric fence.

"Don't stop seeing me," she said.

She kissed me. Her white dress glowed with the ferocity of an atomic bomb.

"I won't," I said. "Okay, I won't."

Two years later I married her in the summer underneath the persimmon trees, and she wore the same white dress as the night she'd climbed through my window. We moved into a small house on the edge of the woods. Neither of us went to college; I took up an apprenticeship as an electrician, she became a sales associate at a small boutique in the center of town.

Though her neurosis hadn't yet begun, I still saw the

seed of it. Even before we were married, she clung to my hips. She paced the house when she got home from work before I did, oftentimes calling my cell phone three or four times to ask if I was okay if I didn't come home at the regular time. She often pressed her face against the window to check if I was walking up the driveway, and several times I saw her silhouette like a lost ghost, the flash of the curtain falling down.

I thought perhaps she needed a distraction.

"What did you want to be as a child?" I asked her one night at dinner.

"I don't know," she said, always the hesitant introvert.

In the distance, the neighbor's dog barked.

"Does he ever keep quiet?" she said.

"There wasn't anything you liked to do?" I asked. "And don't worry about the dog."

"Well," she said, and she set her fork down, as she always did when she spoke about something that was private and could only be extracted from her with precise words, "I used to draw a lot. And paint. I always liked doing that."

"Why did you stop?"

"I don't know," she said, "why does anyone?"

So I built her a small studio up in the attic, set up an easel, canvases, a box of oil paints, a desk with sketchpads and graphite pencil, a work lamp. I knocked out part of a wall and built her a window. It seemed to work for a little while. She still paced the floor, but at night instead of clinging to me until I finally collapsed to go to bed she'd stay up in the studio for a few hours drawing or painting. Nothing special, flowers or the red barn on the other side of the street, children with button eyes and disproportionate limbs. The important thing was that it kept her occupied for a while.

But one day I came home and she was nowhere to be found - not standing by the window or pacing the floor or upstairs in the studio. I went down into the kitchen and called her cell phone. No response. I figured she had been caught up at work, so I crossed the kitchen about to open the refrigerator. That's when I heard her scream.

I ran to the back door, grabbing the first thing that I could think of, a wrench sitting on the counter that I'd used to fix the washing machine.

"June!" I called. I couldn't see her out there - and the From behind the fence, she screamed again.

I jumped over the fence and found her face down in the dead winter grass and the neighbor's dog tearing at her back, biting into her neck. Blood ringed the dog's muzzle, a strip of her sweater hooked into his teeth.

"June!"

She made a rasping noise as if trying to call out for me, and the dog stepped on the back of her head with one paw, pushing her face further into the dirt. I ran across the field with the wrench held tightly in my fist.

When I got close enough the dog turned toward me, snarling. I saw the rabies foam in its muzzle and when he lunged at me I hit him in the side of the head with the wrench. He wailed and fell into the grass with the force of the blow. I hit him over and over again until he was dead.

That night in the hospital the nurses had to hold June down as she got shot after shot into her stomach. I held her hand and she turned her head from side to side with sick sweat on her forehead. Her back and neck were covered gaping holes of gore.

"He took my wings," she kept saying, "that dog took my wings. I'll never get better now."

"It'll be over soon," I said.

Even in her delirium, she insisted she keep the sweater and mend it, though I could never wash out the blood.

It got worse after that. She quit her job because she saw rabid dogs lurking everywhere, in bushes and back alleyways and in the eyes of customers. She refused to go out into the backyard or in the field where she'd gotten bit. Instead she stayed in the house trying to stick her fingers through the nylon sutures in her neck. She stopped going up into her studio to paint or draw, and wouldn't tell me why - perhaps because even in the innocuous paintings of children and flowers she saw herself reflected back, and in herself she saw the virus and the rabid dog.

She clung to me with a new ferocity. Consolation meant nothing. If I wasn't in the room, stuck to her, then it meant that I must be in the back field, face down in the dead grass, a wild creature tearing my wings out. Or that at any moment a dog might bust through the window, spraying glass across the living room, and set in to devour her. When we had sex she did it quietly, focused, her arms wrapped around me and her red hair dripping down over my eyes. She rocked on top of me with the steady rhythm of a hypnotist, not with pleasure, but with mechanics, as if she could seduce me with squeezed hips and sweat to never leave her side.

"Only two people die of rabies a year in the entire country," I said. "You're going to be fine."

"It could've been me," she said. Then she turned and pulled up her mended sweater that she refused to get rid of, the bloodstains still clearly visible on her back, and showed me the scars on her shoulder blades.

"It was me."

That was when the round of psychiatrists and therapists started. I took her to every place within three hours of our town that I could find. They sat her down on half a dozen couches and extracted the gray matter from her brain. They got her to reveal more to them than she'd ever revealed to me. She feared abandonment because two of her siblings had died, and her mother divorced twice. Not to mention the dog. They lay her childhood out on a map, dosed her with drugs, talk sessions, systematic desensitization.

In response she withdrew further into herself, and started to stand in the open threshold with her hand held out in front of her, waiting.

When I thought about leaving, I thought of her in the translucent white dress, her arms snarled in the branches of the tree. Somehow the image kept me running up the driveway every day for three years to take her hand and lead her back inside.

I will tell you a secret now, the terrible and ugly truth about our neuroses. Our parents and our lovers will tell us that we are afraid of nothing, in order to dispel our fear. They will try to convince us that the dark outside will never crawl through the windows and drape itself over our beds. No, dear, you will never find a rattlesnake in your sleeping bag. Don't worry; nobody is looking at you when your limbs become hot wires and you trip over the furniture. Hell, you probably already know what I'm going to tell you.

June got bit again.

My car broke down on the way home and I didn't get

back until late at night. When I finally did manage to get home I didn't find June standing at the threshold of the door with her arm outstretched. I thought immediately of that moment over three years ago, when I'd found her in the field out back with the rabid dog. My pace quickened. When I got to the house I found the front door open and the wind howling through the living room like a cave. One of the corners of the rug was upturned. When the wind lifted I smelled a tepid, coppery smell.

"June?" I called out.

A gasp in response.

I turned on the lights and found June draped over the upturned couch, a lamp shattered at her feet, her chest cracked open, half her face torn. The blood pooled into her navel and congealed in her hair. I ran to her. Knelt and tried to feel a pulse.

"Oh god, June," I said.

She coughed and spit up blood all over me. Her eyes shot open.

"He bit me again," she whispered.

She closed her eyes and became still.

This time in the hospital the nurses didn't have to hold her down for her shots, as she was barely conscious. I kept asking "Is she going to be okay?" so many times that the doctor with the sloping jaw and cat-shaped birthmark on his face asked me to go out into the waiting room. When the doctor came out I cornered him, wringing my hands so hard I thought I might break my wrists.

"She has several broken bones, a punctured lung," the doctor said, "multiple lacerations in her back and throat. We've done the best we could."

I swallowed hard. If I had her white dress then, I would've pressed it again my nose and mouth.

"So she's not going to make it?"

"We think she'll be fine," he said. "We've stabilized her."

I laughed.

"Then what was that bullshit about 'we've done the best we could'?" I said, and laughed again, heady, timorous. "You're a sick fuck."

Much to my surprise, the doctor's face broke out in a smile.

"Can't disagree with you," he said.

June stayed in the hospital for seven days. On the eighth day they called me and told me that she could go back home. When they wheeled her out of the hospital in a wheelchair to come meet me in the carport, June was smiling underneath all her bruises and cuts.

"How are you?" I asked. I bent down to hug her. She brushed her crooked mouth against my cheek.

"I feel fine," she said. "It doesn't hurt anymore."

When I drove her home I expected her to be limp and sluggish. Yet she kept her head erect against the car seat, and her eyes open. They were bright and ferocious, brighter than I'd ever remembered.

"Are you sure you're fine?" I asked.

She smiled at me and in that smile I thought I saw the hint of a cold thing, something I couldn't quite pin down. Cold like crossing a tile floor barefoot in the middle of the night. Cold like the slick branches of a bending tree.

June healed fast. She stayed in bed for several days, but soon she was able to walk around, though with a slight limp, and even got up and down the stairs. Though the change in her was sudden, at first I didn't recognize it. I suppose that's what happens; you get so caught up in a routine that it's easy to keep living in the dream of it. I thought I should've felt relieved when June stopped waiting at the threshold for me to return, but instead I felt lost, like something inside of June had fled - all ritual gone. In fact, she stopped pacing the floor or waiting by the window like the ghost of the curtains. She even spoke of getting another job.

"I've been thinking about it for a while," she said. "I think it's time for me to get out of the house again."

"Wait a while," I said, looking at the ruin of her face, "you still need a lot of time to heal."

She consented to staying in the house, though she took to spending all of her time up in the studio that she hadn't touched in three years. Several times I'd wake up in the middle of the night to find she still hadn't come to bed. I often rolled over and climbed up the attic ladder to find her at the canvas wearing her bloody sweater, head bent down to the brush, red hair alive,

"It's four in the morning," I said, "you must be tired."

"Oh? I didn't notice."

She kept painting, without looking back at me.

Her subjects turned darker and more abstract. She stored away the flowers and children of three years ago and started to paint mechanical creatures, black spheres, spurts of red color that bubbled out of what appeared to be a crack in the universe. She painted amorphous shapes underneath a red moon. I saw her floating across space, and I was unable to follow.

A few weeks later when we went back to the hospital to get x-rays, the doctors found her bones completely healed.

"What god are you praying to?" the doctor with the cat

birthmark asked June. "I think I need to switch religions."

June, sitting on the edge of the examining table in her paper gown, only smiled her cold smile.

When we got home that night she followed me into the bedroom. When I started to undress she grasped my hips from behind and blew cool air into my ear. I found myself unable to move for a few moments, caught in her grip as if encased in a wild tree.

"June?" I asked.

"I feel so strong," she said. "Like I could do anything."

"What's happened to you?"

She guided me to the bed and pulled my shirt up over my head.

"Do you really want to know?" she asked.

"Yes," I said, "I want to know."

She straddled me and touched her face that was no longer a ruin, but a mass of pink scars quickly fading. Before she spoke she bent down and uttered a low, soft growl.

"I don't need you anymore," she said.

One night while drifting off to sleep June woke me by appearing by my side and whispering in my ear.

"I'm going out," she said.

Half asleep, thinking I was in a dream, I rolled over and kissed her on the cheek.

"You don't go out," I said.

"The person you used to know wasn't me."

She left. I went to sleep but couldn't break the cold. I dreamed of her when she was sixteen and nursing the owl that died in her backyard. She scooped it up in her arms and rocked it, whispered hush hush, whispered, "I don't know how to help you." She wore her white dress, but it was spattered with blood.

Several hours later I awoke to a presence standing in the doorway of the bedroom. I sat up in bed and saw a silhouette standing in the gray light, three-quarter moonlight sweeping over the floor and soaking into her skin.

"June?"

Without speaking, she crawled into bed beside me and curled up to sleep. I put my arms around her and pressed my face into her hair. She smelled of something musty and thick that I couldn't quite place.

"Where have you been?" I asked.

In response she only stretched out her body and went to sleep in my arms. I stayed awake for a long time after that, overwhelmed by the smell that emanated from her.

In the morning I found the bed covered in blood and bird feathers. June was gone.

I gathered up the bed sheets to put in the wash, finding it difficult to breathe or swallow as I did so. I called June's name, but there was no response. I went into the kitchen, stuffed the sheets into the washer trying not to gag, and turned the machine on. When I went into the living room to look for her I found the front door wide open.

I found June on the porch, leaning against the railing with her hair wrapped around her wrists.

"What happened last night?" I asked.

"What do you mean?" she asked.

"Where did you go?" I said. "Why is there blood and feathers in our bed?"

"I was looking for him," she said.

"Who's him?"

Though she didn't turn around, I felt her smile. I felt its thin chill spread from her to me.

"The dog that bit me."

"What were you planning on doing when you find him?"

She turned around and strode toward me. She grabbed the back of my head and kissed me hard enough to bruise. Her eyes were about to swallow the world.

"Bite him back," she said.

A thin line of drool ran down her chin. I watched it spill past the cusp of her lip and drip down onto her sweater. I grabbed her shoulders and pushed her back. She laughed as I did it, caught the balcony rail behind her and leaned backwards over the edge until her feet lifted off the ground.

"So this is what you're doing?" I asked her. "You're trying to somehow personify the dog that bit you? You think that by changing into him you'll somehow defeat him? Leave feathers and blood in our bed?"

She leaned even further over the balcony, lifting her legs up in the air, and laughed and laughed.

"I'm taking you to the doctor."

"You don't understand," she said. "I'm better than I've ever been. If only you could see."

"You're delusional."

Instantly she pulled herself up on the balcony, her face set into a sneer.

"You would think that."

"What are you even talking about?" I said, "I just want to help you."

"You just want your scared little girl back," June said, and she tossed her hair behind her shoulders. "You want quiet little June stiffening underneath the persimmon trees. Shivering, wings torn out. Waiting for you to come home. Your pet."

"June," I whispered. I touched her shoulder.

"Don't touch me," she said. She shrugged me off her and went back inside.

For a long time I sat on the porch with my head on my hands. When I did go back inside, I heard June walking around in her studio upstairs. I made dinner for her that night, but she never came down to eat. At about one in the morning, I hauled myself off the kitchen chair, washed the dishes, and went to bed.

At four in the morning she came into the bedroom and crawled on top of me. Her presence woke me up. I felt lucid, but my depth perception seemed off. The quality of the objects around me took on an extra dimension, as if I'd woken up from a dream into a deeper dream.

"Hey," she said.

She stretched her body out over mine. Nuzzled my neck. She smelled the same as she did the night before, that heavy, musty smell.

"June," I said, "you need help."

In response she pulled my shirt above my head.

"June," I said.

She kissed my stomach, her red hair hiding her face. Each movement was jagged.

"Please stop," I said, "we need to talk about this."

I grasped her chin and pulled her head up toward mine. I couldn't see any features of her face except for that smile. I recoiled from it, and found myself with my hands out and away from her, my back flat against the headboard. She moved forward and trapped me against the headboard by grabbing it with both hands on either side of my head. She growled and ground her hips against me.

I turned my face away from her. Almost gently, she dug her nails into my chin and tried to pull me toward her. She kissed me on the cheek. Then the side of my mouth. When I didn't respond, she growled again, pressed our bodies closer. Her sweater clung to my throat.

I tried to speak her name, but when I opened my mouth there was only the heat of her lips, her tongue trying to push its way in. Her limbs were like a cage. When she breathed, the gridiron tightened around me. When I continued to resist, she used her other hand to squeeze my throat.

I gasped and couldn't get any air. The room danced with spots of exploding color. I grabbed the hand choking me, but couldn't peel it away.

I did the only thing I could think of to do - I parted my lips and let her inside.

She loosened her grip on my throat, but didn't completely relinquish it. I inhaled a rush of air and she kissed me again, deeper. I wanted to attempt to pull away again, but the reminder of her hand still on my throat made me go limp. She drew me into her, and I responded, choking softly in the back of my throat, tasting the blood on her tongue.

After a moment, she drew back.

"Oh," she said, and laughed low, "you're hard."

She snapped her head toward the window. I flinched.

"Wow, it's so bright outside. Can't you see that moon? It's beautiful."

She let go of my throat, jumped off the bed, and ran out into the hallway. A few seconds later I heard the back door open and slam shut.

"June!"

I scrambled out of bed and chased her. I ran into

the kitchen and wrenched the door open, and though I couldn't see the fence out in the dark I knew where it was. I vaulted myself over it and dropped down into the field on the other side.

"June! Where are you?"

I ran blindly out into the field, the dark thick on my eyes, my limbs, turning my heart into sludge. I couldn't see anything, much less where June went, but I almost thought that I could smell her, blood and feathers, thick on the still, winter air. I ran with the night beating on my back and my head, the night slurring on my shoulder like a drunk. I knew when I passed the place where the dog first attacked June, because I touched down barefoot on the impression his head made when I bashed it into the ground. Or so I thought. Perhaps I'd run past that place long ago. I no longer knew where my feet started and the ground ended. In the dark everything transformed into a single, solid mass.

Sometimes I asked myself if I truly loved the girl in the white dress standing outside my window, or if instead I loved the quiet cool place that occupied the space of her, still enough to see my own reflection. That is the curse many of us carry, I think: we wander the earth looking for ourselves and instead we find the quiet girls, the looking-for-love girls, and we fill the blank spaces with who we think they should be.

I don't know why I thought about this while I ran. Maybe because in the dark there were no blank spots to fill, only this boiling night, scar-tissue night, and for the first time I could strip away the lunatic sculptures that June and I constructed in those years together, now leaving nothing but space.

But like I said before, I was never good at thinking about things like that.

As I continued to run my eyes adjusted to the darkness and the gray shapes of trees loomed at me from the distance. Then the moon flared from behind their heavy branches. That was the first time I'd truly noticed it - the moon. How could I have not seen it? The full moon, bearing its weight down on the trees, bursting bright. A maniacal eye.

"June!"

I collapsed beneath the tree line. My ribs burned with the strain. My lungs beat at my bones as if to escape. I grasped chunks of dirt and grass between my hands and I wanted to stand up but the terrible pressure of the moon kept me low. The moon spilled out of my mouth and the moon spilled out over my back, striking and biting and chewing and dripping. I crawled to get away. I reached for anything that I could think of - roots, poison white mushrooms, rye, more dirt, as if they were relics that would protect me.

That's when she screamed.

Underneath my breath I whispered, "Not again."

The moon lifted its paralyzing hands off of me, and I jumped up off the ground and ran in the direction of her scream. Not far. Somewhere in these trees. This time I didn't have a wrench. I gritted my teeth as I ran. I'd use my bare hands. I'd drive my thumbs straight through that rabid dog's eyes until I touched the brainstem.

But when I found her, there was no dog to be seen.

She crouched in the grass in the fetal position, head buried and her hands clutching fistfuls of her hair.

The moon sank its teeth into her. Even the trees turned insidious. Their limbs were like knives. I moved toward her.

"June?" I said. "What's happening to you?"

"Don't," she said when I got close, "go away."

"You know I love you," I said, "tell me what's going on."

She screamed again. Her hands shook. She held onto her head like it might burst and rocked herself in the dirt. I moved a little closer.

"Let me take you home. It'll be okay. We'll go to a doctor."

"No!" she said.

She started to change.

Only a bad dream, I thought, when her skin unraveled itself from her fingers and her bloodied sweater burst in two at the back. Any moment I would find myself back in my room at the age of sixteen, and when I heard the rapping at my window and looked out the window there would be nothing but my own reflection. I wouldn't need a girl in white to justify myself. I wouldn't need to pretend-

-But oh, how vividly I saw the bristling black fur emerging from her skin. How tangible the elongating of her limbs, her skull splitting in two and the rabid bones, snout and muzzle and sleek new animal casement. I almost tasted the claws that kicked out of her fingers and feet and scrabbled at the dirt. My small June, growing bigger and bigger and bigger.

I found myself taking several steps back. But before I could move far, June, or what used to be June, hurled herself across the distance and shoved me against a nearby tree. The force of it threw my neck back, and when I hit the trunk of the tree sharp pain flooded into my spine. She opened her mouth, now large enough to stick my head inside and I saw the sharp rows of dog teeth with the canines glittering in spit.

"Oh June," I whispered.

She lifted her head up and howled. I shrank against the tree. Inside of her I could not see the girl with the white dress, the girl with desperate sex holding her hand outstretched across the threshold of the door. There was only this enormous body with the rabies spittle - no, not rabies, her own special virus - flying out of her mouth and her limbs swinging outwards growing larger, crushing the girl skeleton beneath its bulk.

I could do nothing but go limp as she encircled my waist with one clawed hand and squeezed. I thought I might burst out of my skin. Nothing left of me but what she wanted, not the man who wanted to push her away a hundred times, a thousand, the one who muttered "go away" underneath his breath while she rocked on top of me in her lulling need. Not the one who built her an elaborate cage full of paints up in the attic to keep her away, told her "you need something else besides me in your life." There was only the me of this moment - ribcage about to pop, chest a landing pad for her teeth, wondering where the gentle scared girl went, missing something about who she used to be but not quite sure what.

God, how strong she was now. Nobody I ever knew. In my ear she growled a low growl. Spit dripped onto my face.

"June."

She squeezed tighter and her claws dug into my skin, puncturing. I coughed, barely able to breathe. I grabbed one of June's enormous claws, and sucked in enough air to speak.

"Why are you mad at me?" I asked, my voice a rasp. "You know I couldn't have done anything for you."

When I closed my eyes red phosphenes exploded on my

eyelids. The moonlight slithered down through the trees and tattooed itself on the back of my brain. I felt the thing that used to be June release me from her grip. My eyes snapped open and she lumbered several steps back. Her eyes, pale and cloudy, wrestled with my face. Wrestled with the moon.

She ran.

"Hey! Come back!" I called out, but there was no response except for the crashing of the trees and her lonely howl, echoing from half a mile away.

I didn't know what else to do - I walked back through the darkened field, climbed over the fence and went back into the house. When I came back, I found myself shaking uncontrollably and unable to stop, like someone had stuck a live wire through my head from ear to ear. I couldn't swallow. Could hardly breathe. I went into the bathroom and pulled off my shirt and found the ragged, red claw marks. Only then did the sharp pain strike me, and I grabbed a bottle of iodine and splashed it across my ribs. As I burned I paced the living room floor. I peered out the curtains. I kept picking up the phone to call the police, but then I'd laugh and shake my head and put the phone down, only to come back several moments later and pick it up once more.

The night clamped down on the house and maybe in that moment I felt what she felt, trapped inside the house with a rabid dog in every periphery. Trapped inside her head in the white dress unable to breathe, training her hips to be a hypnotist's pendulum, pulling off the bloody sweater to look back in the mirror at the wings she lost and perhaps never had.

I climbed up into her attic studio and I looked out the

window. I looked for her but I could only see the dark field and the moon and the tops of trees and the reflection of my head pressing against the glass stirring sinking spit on my chin, claw marks and kisses leaving burns on the glass. I went to sleep curled up on the floor of the attic and I dreamed of winter storms, but what fell from the storm clouds wasn't rain, but dead owls. They littered the lawn and the field and the roof, all facing up, necks broken, eyes open. My eyes.

And I dreamed of her.

I woke to the hazy morning and a dog barking. I glanced toward the window and I saw sunlight streaming through. Suddenly last night seemed unreal, but when I moved I felt the ache in my bones and the cuts from her claw marks. With slow, deliberate motions I got up off the floor and climbed down the attic stairs. I went into the kitchen, the dog still barking outside. Then I went into the living room, crossed the floor, and peeled back the curtains.

I found her outside lying on the porch. I ran to the front door, yanked it open, and ran out toward her. June lay on her back, naked. Gore streaked her hair and fingernails and mouth. I bent down to check her breath. When I did so, she coughed and her eyes fluttered open.

"June, what happened?"

"I bit him back," she said. "I got him good."

She touched her hair and left red streaks on her hands. Quivering, she lay her hands back down and turned her head toward the wooden porch floor. A smile splayed across her face.

I picked her up and she wrapped her hands around my neck. She buried her head in my chest. I carried her to the car parked at the end of the gravel road.

"Where are you taking me?" she asked as I maneuvered her to open the car door

"Somewhere safe," I said.

"Love you," she whispered, and kissed my mouth. Closed her eyes. I tasted the caked blood. I put her in the back of the car, gently, so as not to hurt her. Without protest she lay across the backseat and grew still.

"I'm going to get you some clothes," I said. "Stay here, okay?"

I closed the car door and went back into the house.

I took a blanket from the top of the washing machine. After that, for the longest time I stood in the middle of the kitchen, trying to find something to grasp onto, trying to find a stray memory, a stray piece of fabric, to hold onto so I wouldn't fall straight through the floor. I felt myself being pulled outside of my body and the sticky strands of my muscles roping my ghost.

June called my name from outside.

"I'm coming!" I said.

On the way out, I grabbed the wrench.

"Do you still love me?" she asked as we drove out of the gravel driveway, the blanket draped over her dead-weight ribs.

"I never stopped," I said.

"Where are you taking me?"

"I told you, somewhere safe."

She turned her head and laughed, leaving a sticky trail of blood against the back seat in the shape of her. I drove faster, bit the inside of my mouth, and glanced at the wrench in the passenger's seat. I didn't know where I was going exactly - I passed the hospital in about twenty minutes and got onto the interstate. I kept driving. My hands turned into wrecks. June fell asleep in the back of the car and rolled over, clutching the blanket. And all the time, the wrench like a love crime on the passenger seat, obstructing my view from anything else, the same wrench once long ago cleaned of blood and matted dog hair and viral spit.

I left the town and kept driving down the interstate. The sun rose over the flat horizon, a hot organ. I knew of a place that I'd been too long ago, once on a summer vacation before I'd ever met June or the monster inside of her, before I'd been confined to the three mile space between my work and her outstretched hand. So long since I'd thought of it. A woodland lake, surrounded by miles of trees and hush spaces. It'd be quiet. We'd be alone. Me, my wife, and the wrench.

In the backseat, June coughed. In the rear-view mirror I saw her curl and uncurl her hands. Stiff, trembling hands, the fingernails caked with gore. She bit at her knuckles and whispered my name. For only a second, I saw the sixteen-year-old girl in the backseat, naked underneath the blanket with the white dress, bloody and mangled, tied around her wrists.

At the next exit, I turned the car around and went back home.

I drove back up our gravel driveway and shut off the engine. I sat in the driver's seat for several minutes, shaking, looking at the wrench, looking back at June.

"Where are we going?" June asked me.

Without responding I got out of the car and opened up the back door. I gathered up June's limp body in my arms. Once more she reached up and clasped her arms around my neck. Her head lolled across my chest, smearing blood.

"There's nowhere to go," I said. "We're not going anywhere."

Though I didn't see it, I felt it pressed against my skin. Her cold smile.

The Bad Baby Meniscus

"There is something very wrong with your daughter," the psychiatrist told Mom. This was before the butterfly bit me, before I saw the world in lemon trees and hungry crows and nectar palettes. One day after school she took me to the psychiatrist's office out in the country, with its pale church-steepled walls and white-washed floors. I told Mom then we were all white-washed, even those who didn't know it, especially those who didn't know it. She pursed her lips like she does when she gets angry but doesn't want to show it, and I was about to speak again, to ask her why she was angry, but a young woman with faded out pink highlights and tired tracks for arms came in and said, "Miss Mellie Anderson, the DOCTOR will see you know," pronouncing doctor like DOCTOR, like something heavy and demanding and final. The young woman led us through the labyrinth of doors, all white, and hallways, all white, until we reached the psychiatrist's office where he waited for us inside a room like a womb, sitting on a plush brown armchair surrounded by his books and pictures of faces in clouds. Mom later told Dad the psychiatrist looked like a dead science fiction writer.

He asked me questions.

"Do you have any friends, Mellie?" He asked. He spoke my name like fierce honey.

"No," I said.

"There's nobody at school you talk to? Or at church?"

"No."

At which he would straighten up in his chair like he just heard a shot and his shadow would lengthen on the wall behind him as if stretching out its spine. Meanwhile Mom on the couch beside me looked down at her lap and studied the backs of her hands.

"What do you like to do?"

"Write stories."

"What do you write about in your stories?"

"Things I see. Places I go. Things I don't see. Places I never go."

"Are you scared right now, Mellie?"

"No."

"Do people ever think you act strange?"

"Yes."

"What do they say?"

"That I'm retarded. That I'm weird."

"Do you think you're retarded, Mellie?"

"No," I said, "I scored real high on the placement test. The teacher said I'm a genius and it's okay to be weird if you're a genius."

"What do you want to do when you grow up, Mellie?"

he asked. I wished he'd stop saying my name like that, like fierce honey, like a stern list of everything you don't want to say but you're forced to say anyways. "Do you want to get married?" he asked, "Have children and a nice home so they can play in the yard? Maybe a nice job as a secretary at some big law firm?"

"No," I said, "I don't want to do any of those things."

"What do you want to do, then, Mellie?" the psychiatrist asked, his voice a thin line.

"I want to drink and smoke and bet at the racetrack. I want to wear a hat like Hunter S. Thompson and become an alcoholic like William Faulkner. I want to write hours past midnight and tell people how things really are or more importantly how I think they should be."

"You know that's not a very good life for a proper young lady like yourself, don't you?"

I said nothing.

"Can you smile for me, Mellie?"

On command I bared my teeth for him, extended my lips past my skull. He frowned. I though I somehow did the wrong thing. I never know when to smile and not when to smile. The psychiatrist took Mom out of the room and I sat there on the couch for nearly twenty minutes. I looked at the pictures of the faces in clouds and when Mom and the psychiatrist came back into the room his face was deader than before and Mom didn't have her lips pursed anymore but she sat down beside me silently and I know when Mom is silent she isn't just angry but something is not quite right in her world and therefore not quite right in mine.

"There is something very wrong with your daughter," The psychiatrist told Mom out in the hallway, but to me he said, "Mellie, we're going to help you be like other people."

Then Mom and the psychiatrist drew up plans for my treatment. Mom scheduled a brain scan for the next week. The psychiatrist drew lots of pictures over which Mom nodded and pulled down her face, just like she did when Aunt Demi died. After the funeral in the kitchen of the funeral parlor I heard Mom tell her sister Jeanna that she sure was glad that bitch was dead. People express their grief in different ways.

I sat on the psychiatrist's couch kicking my feet and looking at the faces in the clouds, which seemed to be transmuting from their benign humanity into monsters with pale puffed bodies and Ibis bird beaks. The psychiatrist talked a lot about the nanotech procedure I'd be getting, how after he got my brain and blood samples and a psychological plan drawn up he'd send it off to scientists in a darkcreek lab and they'd engineer nanotech machines to make me all better, which I think meant wanting to get a husband and knowing when to smile in the proper company. Mom said something about how she should have gotten that eugenics procedure when she was younger.

"What's eugenics?" I asked.

"There, there," the psychiatrist said. "Nothing to be ashamed of. There are always unfortunate anomalies, no matter how good the program is. Nothing we can't fix. Just be thankful we got to her when she was still young."

"What's eugenics?" I asked.

Mom said nothing.

When we were in the car on the way back home she started crying and she put her hand on my knee even though I tried to nudge her away. "You know I love you,

Mellie," she said, "Don't you know I love you?"

"Yeah," I said, "I know Mom," but I couldn't help but get to thinking she didn't love me as I was me but the me that I had the potential to become.

I was out in the garden because Mom put on her face like a surgical mask and said, Mellie, me and your father have to talk about grownup things, so I went out back and Mom locked the door behind me and for a moment I watched their silhouettes quicken and speak in bulbous shapes in the kitchen window underneath the paisley curtains before leaving to go to the garden. It used to be Mom's garden, and her rhodenderon and blue roses were still there, but the dandelions were mine, and the weeds were mine, and the red scratched dirt was mine. I dressed my scaredy crow, Harrison Ford, in Mom's purple pants and Dad's plaid flannels. I stuffed his neck with straw. I dreamed of a world where every good man was a scaredy crow, and every good girl drank like William Faulkner and bet on the horses at the racetrack. But the cold hard truth, and that was one of Mom's favorite phrases, the cold hard truth, was that there were only a few places for people like me and Harrison Ford in the universe and those places were for the most part broken gardens and holes in the earth.

"Mellie!" Mom called as she walked out toward the garden, "Mellie, come on inside." I turned away from Harrison Ford toward Mom, tilted my head to my one side in such a way so that my hair fell away from my neck. That's when the butterfly, with flaring orange wings and ferocious brown eye marks, fluttered against me and bit me on the neck. I winced and clapped my hands against the stinging wound as the butterfly flew away, her colorful back screaming like the panic stretches of a bad dream, mouth grotesque, fangs dripping a nausea serum.

Everything got real slow, like I'd just stuck my head underwater and the reeds reached out to tug on my hair and encircle my face. I got the feeling that underwater lived another me, a liquid, luminous blue me, who parted the reeds and struck me on the mouth. I became dizzy and numb and nervous-strained, and when I tried to take a step I collapsed in the dirt. Mom ran over to me and picked me up. She carried me to the house while my eyes grew droopy and shined and I held tightly to the place on my neck where the butterfly bit.

"She got bit by a damn bug playing out in that garden," Mom told Dad.

"I'll get the iodine," Dad said, "Put her on the couch. She looks a little white."

Dad got the iodine and a pink bandage. "Let me see it, Mellie." And when I wouldn't move my hand away because I was afraid my blood would leak away, float away; dissolve right into the hard-smacked mouth of the underwater me, he peeled my fingers back, burned me with the iodine, and slapped on the bandage.

"That looks nasty, Mellie," he said, "Keep it cleaned or it'll get infected."

I didn't really hear, because when I brought my hand up to my face my fingers flaked away like melanin scales.

I read in a book once that labyrinths were once used in rituals to prepare initiates for the experience of death. God is a mathematician. God is a master of equations that split into astronomical, infinite possibilities. Death is God's most precious creation. Death expands from the center outward in the most complex, unending geometric shapes.

Having a brain scan is kind of like that.

The doctor made me strip out of my clothes and put on a blue hospital gown.

"This is the most beautiful blue I've ever seen," I said, pulling the sides of the gown out like wings. The doctor laughed. He noticed the pink bandage on my neck.

"What happened there, Mellie?"

"I got bit by a butterfly," I said. The doctor pulled back the bandage.

"You better treat that," he said, "It looks infected. I can give you some antibiotics."

"You better talk to my Mom," I said, "I don't know anything about that."

"Okay, Mellie," the doctor said, "Hop up here."

The doctor made me get on top of a cold table in nothing but my blue hospital gown, and he said stick out your arm, and I stuck out my arm and he inserted a syringe into a vein in my arm full of special medicine so he could see my brain better. After that he said, "Okay, Mellie," he was always saying, "Okay, Mellie," and then, "Stay real still so we can take a clear picture, Okay, Mellie," and he left the room and the cold table was swallowed up by the CAT machine.

In the dark hollow throat of the CAT machine I saw the face of God. I was not very happy about this.

Back in the waiting room after I'd discarded the beautiful blue and put on my regular clothes Mom said, "Be thankful you weren't born in the dark ages, Mellie. We have the technology to fix this sort of thing now. Why, just fifty years ago we couldn't have done anything to help you. Children like you would run around like dirty animals and be submitted to the most horrible tortures."

"Like what tortures?" I asked. I couldn't imagine anything worse than having your arm stuck with a syringe full of special medicine or being made to sit in the dark for what seemed like hours trying not to move so the doctors could take a good picture.

"Oh, like psychotherapy," Mom said, "Come on dear, let's go. The doctor gave me a prescription for some antibiotics for that bite on your neck."

"And then I won't have to come back," I said.

"No, you'll have to come back for more tests. But it'll be all over before you know it."

"They won't stick me with a syringe again will they?"

"I'm sorry Mellie," Mom said, "We're going to have to draw some blood, and of course when they put the nanomachines in you they'll have to do that with a syringe."

"Nanomachines?"

"Tiny machines," Mom said, "As tiny as your cells. They travel through the bloodstream and they can reproduce just like real cells and can talk to real cells to tell them what to do. They'll repair the damaged tissues in your brain."

"Damaged tissue?"

"Like the dendrites that connect different parts of your brain. The machines will make you normal."

I think in pictures. There's a picture for every word, and normal is the curved crescent meniscus of water in a glass vial, like a barely imperceptible line that separates the water from the air. It's so easy to be a bad and unhappy child because there are so many more frequencies of abnormality than normality. Normal is a finite and rare phenomenon in this universe, but don't let the doctors know that.

Ever since the butterfly bit me whenever I closed my eyes my limbs dissolved like cool metallic dust. Mom gave me an antibiotic tablet every night with a glass of water before I went to bed, but it didn't seem to help. I checked my neck in the mirror and the bite looked vicious and serrated, puffed red at the edges, black and gummy in the center. The pink bandage stayed on. Mom didn't seem to really notice that it wasn't healing, she was more concerned with the matter of my wrongness, and the blood tests and brain tests and psychological evaluations I had to fill out over and over again and the meetings I had to do with my dead science fiction writer psychiatrist DOCTOR.

"We're almost prepared to synthesize your treatment in the labs, Mellie," the psychiatrist said, "Not much longer now. Be patient and this'll all be over soon. Do you have any questions?"

"Yeah," I said, "I have lots of questions."

"Would you like to share?" he asked. Mom sitting beside me looked more grim than usual.

"How come you never asked me if this what I wanted?"

The psychiatrist straightened up in his chair and his face went slack. It seemed like every time I said something I didn't like or he couldn't answer he got shot by some invisible bullet, and right now it was working its way through his silver ballooned stomach, through his dysthymic, inveterate psyche.

"If we don't continue with this procedure, Mellie, you won't be able to function in society. You won't be happy."

"I'd be happy if people stopped telling me how unhappy I must be."

"Mellie," Mom said, "Mellie, you are going to have this procedure."

And so it must be, that I will bury myself beside the rabbit and the dog decomposing in sweltering trash bags underneath the fennel out back.

I am okay with the death of me because I have seen God in the tunnel mouth of a CAT scan machine, and I have traversed a labyrinth full of strange and glass-nailed creatures in preparation for the place I am going, for the hell I am in now. Even in hell I can learn to be happy, I'm sure of it, because what comprises hell is not fire and traitors frozen in Cocytus, but a state of being that can be at the very least tolerated. What comprises the self is more than the head, and more than the heart. It is of something other. Not the soul, not anything like that, but a miasmic essence that like the branches of a trees dips down into your veins and never lets you go.

Welcome to hell, the sign said on the road in, but it doesn't have to be so bad, because you've walked the labyrinth and you know that God is a mathematician and death spirals out forever and even the master creator of the universe can't account for anomalies like you.

The butterfly bite started looking even worse. Its poisonous cat-eye center dripped orange pus and black ichor. If I touched the bite with my finger pain spiked up my neck and made my head throb. I thought the bite looked like the back wings of an Edith's checkerspot butterfly, just like the one that bit me, with fanned out orange and white marks palm flushed against my neck, and a black morass origin. Everything spiraled out from the center. Even the back of a butterfly, and its signature fangbite, contained God's hidden mathematical formula in its geometry. All math, all of nature, butterflies and broken gardens, led back to the labyrinth.

As I slept the butterfly bite stretched and spread its wings. Underwater me came back from the kheb to lay beside me on the bed and open up the ground. Reeds hung from her hair, her fingernails. She smelled like deep dark water. Big day tomorrow, she said, I know you're scared, but you should know that all living matter is in a constant movement toward death. Then she held her hand out to me, and her fingers split at the seams. Butterfly claws, hospital gown blue and iridescent, emerged from the skin.

The next day Mom took me back to the hospital and we didn't see my psychiatrist or get a blood test but instead the young woman with the faded pink highlights and tired tracks for arms took us to a white room with whitewashed walls that looked just like the walls in the hallway, except there was a steel table and a steel counter with butcher weapons laid out on a tray. The silver of those butcher weapons was the only color in the room.

Mom squeezed my hand. She said "I love you, Mellie."

"I love you too, Mom," I said, "I've already said goodbye."

Instead of saying "Oh, Mellie," and shaking her head like she normally did when I said something she didn't understand, she just smiled.

A stranger doctor came in and told me to lie down on the steel table.

"Do I have to put on a gown first?" I asked.

"No, that won't be necessary," he said. I lay down on the table and Mom came over to my side to hold my hand. The butterfly bite flapped its wings in a ferocious rhythm. The ache shot to the back of my head. The doctor made me squeeze my hand, the one that Mom wasn't holding, and he disinfected the skin and swabbed it with a cotton ball.

"Well, Miss Mellie Anderson," I expected the doctor to say, "Let me just inject you with about 25 milliliters of a girl you've never met. Would you like to say any last words? Have you made the proper arrangements with the funeral home?"

But after he found a vein all he said was, "hold still."

"How do you feel?" Mom asked on the way home, even though I knew what she really wanted to ask what, "Do you still feel like drinking and smoking and going to bet at the racetracks? Do you still want to become an alcoholic writer like William Faulkner and wear a crazy hat like Hunter S. Thompson? Do you have any urges to get married and have children, or perhaps become a secretary at a nice law firm? At the very least, Mellie, will you not smile anymore when you're not supposed to smile?"

"I feel dizzy," I said, "Like there are butterflies in my head."

"The doctor said it would take a while for the nanomachines to make their repairs," Mom said, "Don't worry, darling."

"And my neck hurts."

Mom glanced over while she was driving and peeled back the pink bandage.

"Oh dear God honey," Mom said, "I gave you those antibiotics to take. Didn't you take them?"

I nodded.

"That looks horrible," she said.

"I kind of like it," I said.

"We're going to have to go back for another prescription," Mom said, "You've developed an immunity or something."

Back home I went out into the garden. The last graying light arched its back over the tops of houses. I pulled weeds and stuffed them in Harrison Ford's legs, because he was beginning to look a little thin. The dizziness wouldn't go away. Butterflies flitted and spread their backs out on the rhodenderon. I covered my neck. My butterfly bite pulsed.

I am undergoing metamorphosis and I can't even feel it. The universe is diminishing and I can't even feel it.

Mom called me back inside and her and Dad and I ate dinner, which was yellow rice and chicken masala, and I couldn't help but notice Mom and Dad seemed happier than usual even though outwardly nothing really changed. I wanted to ask them why they were happy. I wanted to ask them what their underwater selves looked like, if they visited them in the night, if a butterfly had ever bitten them, if now that there were machines in my head everything would be okay. I said nothing.

I couldn't sleep.

Outside in the dark in my broken garden I began to die. Harrison Ford whispered as the wind teased his clothes. I peeled the pink bandage off of my butterfly bite and I curved my back toward the stars. My limbs dissolved. I closed my eyes and my eyelids dissolved. My skin broke beneath melanin scales. My mouth trailed off into nectar dust. I hoped when I was gone Mom would like her new daughter. I hoped she would smile only when it was appropriate to smile, that she wouldn't want to become a writer or an alcoholic that she wouldn't want to play in a broken garden with a malformed scaredy crow. I hoped she would become married and have children, that she would be everything Mom ever wanted that wasn't ever me.

I was becoming a butterfly. My butterfly claws emerged from the cocoon of my skin. My shoulders split and slimy, newly formed butterfly wings emerged from my back. I floated off the earth. I couldn't set my feet. Couldn't stop the inevitable dissolution of everything that ever existed.

I hoped that the butterfly that took my skin prepared herself in the labyrinth. That she knew what was coming as I fade. As I fade.

The Singing Grass

I told him that in the singing grass I saw a deer tear out the heart of a cougar, but instead of staying away he went out there to paint. He didn't want to believe me about the deer, but he didn't want to believe that I was a virgin either, so I let it go. It wouldn't matter how many times I described the way I knelt at the edge of the singing grass, barefoot and tearing at my dress, eyes shaking like psychotropic leaves. And it wouldn't matter how I described the raw mass of heart quivering on the ground at my feet, the deer on the other side of the meadow licking the blood off her muzzle with her black-tipped tongue.

And all the while the grass, the blue aberrant grass, singing to lure me over the edge, press my face into its depths and drown me.

Because I said to him once, when we first met, "all writers are liars," like a badge of honor, and I've never managed to escape it since.

So I stopped trying to stop him from going up there. Instead I watched him from my hiding place in the cover of the trees as he carried his painting supplies out of town to the side of the mountain, past the woods and the angry, gray-bottomed spring and then finally, the meadow on the edge of the singing grass.

He didn't paint landscapes outside on the edge of the singing grass, at least, not the kind of landscapes you see on bathroom walls and in the sterile, white-proofed halls of psychiatric wards. What he painted was alien and uncomfortable, anthropomorphic beings with exposed nerves and melting skin, balloons like vats filled with saline and brains. He painted clowns with holes for eyes and bodies made for flatworms, apocalyptic fog, empty skies that crackled like static.

I'd never liked to watch people make art before, but I watched him paint because there was something alluring and impractically aesthetic about the way he moved, like an underwater machine. Even if I closed my eyes I'd still be able to feel his movement, the shadow of it, and all angles of him digging a hole into gravity.

"I saw you watching me the other day," he told me one night when we went back home. "You were watching me from the grass." He slouched in a chair in the corner of the room underneath a portrait of his last ex-girlfriend, flowers spurting out of her decapitated head. He looked up at me with bug eyes that bit like teeth and he smiled.

But the girl he saw in the grass wasn't me.

I remember as a child I went out to the singing grass with a notebook and I'd write what I saw like it mattered, poetry about love and other abstract concepts I had no real understanding of, journal entries about the friends I made up. I didn't know what the singing grass meant back then, or what it contained, but it drew me to it anyways. I thought the blue grass looked like mammoth skin, and in the night when the full moon came out to the meadow I thought it was silently conversing with the dirt below.

Out on the edge of the singing grass I learned the rules. When you're a writer, you can only use words like serpentine and aberrant once in a lifetime. "So" and "very" are pointless modifiers. The road to hell is paved with adverbs. If you ask your friends to read your work, they'll never tell the truth.

And if you're artistic and attractive and enigmatic, people will fall in love with you at the most inconvenient of times.

Keep reading, that wasn't the most important part. As a child out on the edge of the singing grass I met the girl that sprung from the earth, the girl with the sewed-on jaw and Morpheus eyes and thin line of drool running down her chin. Her clothes gleamed with moths tied into the fabric, still alive. Snakeskins hung intertwined in her hair, and she clutched to her waist a formaldehyde jar full of black arms.

"What are you working on there?" she asked when she saw me. Her voice was the voice of glass and mulch.

I said nothing. My pen hovered over the page of my notebook. When I swallowed my throat felt like the blades of a meat grinder.

"Can I read?" she said.

I closed my notebook and shook my head. I didn't mean to; it was nothing but a reflex. Even in the face of something alien I tried to hide my unfinished work. And I knew she was alien. No girl from the town could've snapped her head back until it touched the tip of her spine. No, she emerged out of the singing grass, out of the electric song that whipped through the meadow and straight through me.

"That's too bad," she said. "Can I show you something?"

She set the formaldehyde jar down in front of her. The wind blew through the singing grass and it started to keen. The noise swept through the girl, into her snake hair and gleaming clothes, in and out with her breath, pulsing to the rhythm of the moths beating her wings. She grasped the fabric of her dress in her fists.

"One day we're going to be good friends," she said.

Slowly, she started to lift up the hem of her dress. As she did so, the black arms in the formaldehyde jar stirred. The black fingers pressed against the inside of the glass jar and it tipped over on its side in the singing grass. The fingers kicked, the serrated ends of the arms braced themselves. The jar started to roll toward me.

I ran.

I didn't come back to the singing grass until years later, after I'd met him, the artist, and realized that if I fell in love with him I'd go insane. We met in a coffee shop in town. He hadn't slept for days and I could see it in his face, the purple-rimmed eyes, and the slack, paralyzed skin. He was holding an art show there. I wanted to impress him because his art somewhat intimidated me, but I couldn't think of anything to say except, "did you know it takes 100,000 years to cross the galaxy at the speed of light?"

At least, that's the romantic version. I don't want to tell you the truth, because it would disappoint you.

But picture this. One night he invited me out for drinks

and I felt sociable, so I went. The next thing I know I've downed two Long Island's, a beer, a shot of vodka with cranberry and I'm staring at his face, which I've never really seen before until now. Not just staring at it, but swimming in it. I noticed his eyes for the first time, bug eyes, always telling a story. His eyebrows that can't stay still, the gaps between his teeth. That was the first time I'd found him attractive, not just in an aesthetic way, but in that intrinsic, warm-blooded sort of way.

"Let's go to the cemetery," I told him. "I'm a necrophiliac. Let's go."

And so we got in his car and drove away from the bar, down into the bottomed-out woods where the trees clamp down like bear traps. We parked beside the cemetery gate and when I got out I saw the silhouette of the mountain leaning over the cemetery.

"Have you ever been up there?" I asked.

"No," he said, "pick a grave so we can start digging."

The next thing I knew I was up in a tree, the tree of life, with his head between my knees and my underwear in the pocket of his jacket. I grasped onto the limbs above my head, or at least, I tried to; they shook with the rain, slippery, like caught birds. I slipped. He caught me and brought me down into the dirt.

"Where did you come from?" he asked me.

"The tree," I said. I started to take off his jacket, then his shirt. He started to do the same to me. That's when I remembered I was a virgin.

"Really? You're joking," he said.

"I wish," I said.

"Are you saving it or something?" he asked.

"No," I said. "I don't know. I've been busy."

"You're lying," he said. "Really?"

"What's with all the questions?"

He took my throat in his hand and squeezed gently, not in a sexual way, more like in the way one holds a puppy by the neck to pick her up. When he kissed me I kept my eyes open. When he took the condom out of his pocket I clasped my knees together.

"You're tense," he said. "Come here."

Because I remembered the girl I'd seen years ago in the singing grass on the side of the mountain.

Now with the mountain looming over the graves, illuminating the graves, a hazy O-ring of fog splitting the distant meadow into shades of purple haze, I thought those memories might make me never sleep again.

Forget this. I'm not good at describing things like this. I don't understand why these mechanical motions have to mean anything, how the aesthetics of this particular setting could mean anything. We could've been picnicking on the moon, drinking strychnine tea in my grandmother's bathtub, it wouldn't have made a damn difference.

He told me once that love was a temporary chemical imbalance. That love turns into hate. Not that any of that is profound, so instead of talking, let's rewrite every love scene in every cheap paperback ever written, turn it into a chemistry lesson so we can watch the violent reactions underneath a sterile glass slide. It won't be difficult to do.

At the end of it all I lay in the dirt underneath the tree of life with my dress hiked up over my hips and condom thrown onto the ground. And still a virgin. I couldn't help it, I started to laugh.

"Why are you laughing?" he asked me.

"No reason," I said.

He cocked his head, raised one eyebrow.

"I lost my nerve," he said.

After that he drove me out of the cemetery and to my home in town. He hugged me like we were chaste, which, I suppose we still were. He took a cigarette out of his jacket pocket. Lit it.

"I'll see you later," he said, voice scratched with smoke.

I didn't go home that night.

Instead, when he drove me away I went back to the meadow, past the woods and the spring, to the edge of the singing grass that I hadn't been to since I was a child. It was just as I remembered. The O-ring around the mountain dissipated, and the side of the sheer rock reached down toward the meadow like a drinking crane.

Don't ask me why I came back. The answer wouldn't satisfy you. Just know that someone must've seen it coming, because the place had been prepared for me.

On the edge of the singing grass sat an upholstered chair from my living room. And next to the chair, my floor lamp.

If I didn't know what I was doing as a writer I would say, "as if in a dream." Because that's what writers say when they don't want to take the time to explain things in a logical way, or they've forgotten the reason why. But sometimes, in real life, there is no causal explanation for the actions that we take. And so, as if in a dream I crossed to the edge of the grass and I sat down in my chair. When I turned on the lamp, though there was no way it should've turned on, the deer grazing in the middle of the singing grass looked up at me. Her eyes gleamed in the light. Behind her I saw

174

the shape of the cougar, almost amorphous, crouching in the grass.

This time I didn't look away from what was about to happen. Blame the intoxication, the particulars of the circumstance, the moonlight striking the grass just so like the bad mood lighting for a budget horror movie. I tensed in my chair and dug my nails into the arms until they bent, but I didn't run.

When the cougar pounced, the deer turned around and struck him. He hit the grass, stunned, and she bent down and ripped out his heart.

The deer glanced up at me, saw me looking at her, and fled.

I crawled through the grass as it keened. I knelt in front of the body of the cougar and watched its heart, still quivering, lit by my lamp that had somehow ended up on the side of a mountain. I tasted its pulse on the tip of my tongue.

My hands shook as I reached out for the heart. It was warm and textured like a tongue, and as I cupped it in my palms it spit out the last of its convulsions and lay still. I brought the heart to my mouth and drew a deep breath. Its viscous, copper smell touched the back of my throat.

I ate the heart.

I think that's when I realized this was never my story.

One day out in the meadow he started to paint her. Even before her outline took shape on the canvas,

I knew he was painting her. I could tell by the colors he mixed. That snake green. Moth brown. The sick gray of her skin. I watched from the trees, my usual hiding place. My chair and lamp had disappeared from the meadow long ago, to be replaced by the artist and his accouterments. The grass shifted its song when he worked here, no longer a keen but a hollow rustle. It drank him in and waited for the time when it could spit him back out.

"What are you working on?" I asked him one night. I'd go over to his house most nights, climb through his open window and onto his bed. I told him at first it was so my boyfriend wouldn't catch me here. But we broke up soon enough and I still went through the same routine.

In truth, I just liked climbing through the window.

Instead of responding, he asked me, "Have you ever heard of quantum entanglement?"

"What?" I asked him.

"Do you know anything about quantum physics?" he asked me.

"Yeah," I said, "The Planck constant. Energy is proportionate to its frequency."

"Quantum entanglement. Two particles can have a relationship even when they're separated by miles."

Even time. Change the state of one particle, and the other one knows what's happening."

"So you could use quantum entanglement to time travel?"

"Sort of," he said. "Yes. But maybe not in the way that you know it."

"What do you mean?" I asked.

He lapsed into silence, outstretched one of his arms so that I could huddle close. He did that often; would go quiet if I asked about the underlying fundamentals of a thing, or would talk about something completely unrelated. That's what happens when you forgetting you're writing a story and you think you're going to be profound. You ask questions trying to get to the center, like the answer will lead you to some ultimate revelation, the perfect Platonic form.

If there was anything important I learned it was this: he taught me how to see a thing for what it is and not what I thought it represented. Not every atom has to be torn apart to get to its nucleus. Not every fact or idea has to be labeled and put in a schema. No, here is the earth that I'm gripping between my fingers. Here is the heart I'm chewing apart. Here is the rattlesnake tied to my wrist and the sharp pain that follows.

Here is the tornado, god of entropy, tearing the house apart, and all I can think is that he looks sexy when he's bent over a broken mirror snorting MDMA through a dollar bill. Everything else is extraneous.

He painted her in profile, with the snakes in her hair writhing as if they were still alive. Her Morpheus eyes became empty slaughterhouses that caved inside her head and then collapsed. The moths sewn onto her dress turned into little children.

It should've ended there, but of course it didn't.

He elongated the bones of her face and stretched out her skin. He gave her a muzzle and a cold black nose tipped with white and a thin line of a mouth. He painted her skin taut and brown and dull. Her dress melded into her bones and on her back he painted spots of white.

Then he ringed her mouth with a rusted red.

On the nights when he couldn't sleep sometimes he crawled onto the bed and leaned over me while I slept. Then he watched, waiting for me to wake up and see him. He touched my face then with both hands, his face stoic.

"What's wrong?" I asked him.

"Nothing's wrong," he said, "just go back to sleep."

I felt the cougar heart in my stomach about to spill out my mouth and nose. It had stayed a part of me all the while, chewed up but indigestible, keening inside of me like the singing grass. I turned my head away and his hands fell. I went to sleep dreaming of being eaten alive.

When he was almost finished with the painting I went back to the singing grass alone one night. She watched me as I walked, I knew she did, like a barefooted changeling from the trees with her hair bending own to flay me.

This time all the furniture from my house waited out on the singing grass. Everything except the walls. There were chairs, bed, shower and sink, the refrigerator, the living room television, the desk from the hallway corner, all of it strewn out in the meadow.

The formaldehyde jar of black arms lay on my bed. It was my bed, there was no doubt, there were the chipped white bedposts, that was the cover I hadn't replaced in seven-odd years, with its ridiculous pink flowers and faded gray corners.

"What is this place?" I said out loud, knowing she was nearby.

No response. The wind whipped through the grass, and the grass howled.

I approached the black arms, expecting them to jump to life in their shroud of formaldehyde. But they remained still, floating in suspension. I reached out and touched the slick jar.

The girl grasped my hand from behind. I jerked my hand away from the jar and whirled around. She stood there, head cocked, a half-smile on her face. The snakeskins hung from her hair sung like the grass.

In one hand she held a shovel.

"What is this place?" I asked. "And why is all my furniture here?" My voice sounded odd to me, like it was coming up from the ground at my feet instead of my throat.

"I've assembled everything here. Everything you wanted to lose but couldn't."

"Stop being enigmatic," I said.

"Am I?" she asked. "Listen. He'll be here soon. You have to start digging."

"What?"

She held the shovel out to me. Reflexively, I reached out to take it. Grasped the handle. Behind me the black arms stirred. My spine kicked, but I didn't want to turn around to look.

"You're still a virgin, aren't you?" she asked.

"What does that matter?"

"Dig," she said, "or I'll tear your heart out."

She smiled to show me her bloodstained, blunt-cut teeth, and then she turned around and disappeared behind the tree line.

The incident in the singing grass was just one of those things that happened to everyone, wasn't it?

But as I set the shovel to the grass in front of my bureau and started to dig, I knew that wasn't true. If I weren't a writer I wouldn't have come up here with my journal and pen to write down those useless things, or trained myself to see the details in my surroundings. If he wasn't an artist, critical, detail-oriented, maybe he would've believed my story and stayed away. Or even if he did think I was a liar, he wouldn't have come up here to paint. As my hands started to sting from gripping the handle and the sweat welded my hair to my forehead, I thought of him. He was in his room asleep now, most likely, or rebounding off the walls with insomniac mania as the unfinished painting of the girl stored in the corner of the house ballooned in his periphery.

Maybe he was reading about astronomy, the thousand different ways to cross the universe, getting drunk and talking about physics to strangers. Anything but walking up to the singing grass, crossing the singing grass, meeting the eyes of the girl who sprung out of the dirt. Please be anywhere but here, because I couldn't handle him falling apart with me.

My shovel hit something metallic and hard. I set down the shovel and knelt down. I brushed away the dirt until I revealed the contours of the circular object buried underneath the grass.

I lifted up the formaldehyde jar, impossibly large, out of the dirt. Inside the jar was a pair of charred black legs.

I unearthed the rest of the jars soon after that. The feet beside the shower, the torso by my upholstered living room chair. The head I found next to the refrigerator. It was almost unrecognizable as a head, a burnt lump of flesh with a shredded neck. It had no lips, no eyes, and two hooked holes for a nose.

"What now?" I asked, after I set all the jars on my bed beside the jar of black arms. From the girl watching me from behind the tree line, there was no response.

The body parts inside the formaldehyde jars started to move.

I stepped back. The lights arranged on the singing grass burst on. More budget horror movie props, I thought, even when my head threatened to pop off my neck with anxiety. The black arms slammed against the top of the lid and the jar burst. The noxious smell of formaldehyde spilled over me, and the arms crawled toward the jar that contained the feet. I unscrewed the lid. The feet kicked and the jar tipped over, flooding my bed with its chemicals. The arms freed the legs next, which uncurled onto the bed like two dying birds. The head turned inside its prison, gnashed its teeth and grimaced to show me its gray, mottled gums. The jar that contained it cracked and collapsed in on itself.

Amidst the glass and formaldehyde on my bed, the body parts found each other and the skin, that black, burnt skin almost unrecognizable as something once human, sewed itself together into what it used to be.

The broken entity on my bed lay flat on its back. Its head sunk down into the bedspread, arms and legs splayed out. He opened his lipless mouth, and he spoke to me with a crumbling tongue.

"You're tense," he said, "Come here."

I paused. My bones shuddered.

"You're him," I whispered.

"Come here," he said once more. His voice softened. "It's been too long."

For once the singing grass laid hush around us. My furniture loomed up like fighting animals, and the air crystallized. I had to push through solid matter to take a step, another step. I broke frozen particles on my skin to climb into the bed. He outstretched his arms. I crouched on top of him.

"Quantum entanglement?" I asked.

"Something like that," he said, "if it helps you to wrap your head around this."

He undressed me with those burnt fingers. Languidly,

like we were touching each other underwater.

Those motions were no longer mechanical and awkward, as they had once been back in the cemetery, but purposeful, almost vicious. I dug my fingers into his cracked shoulders, and when I looked down into his eyeless sockets I didn't laugh. I didn't look away.

When I was naked he rolled me over on my back, on top of the broken glass and pool of

formaldehyde. He spread my legs apart and penetrated me in one fluid motion. I cried out.

"It'll hurt less the next time," he said, and he touched my face. My hands squeezed into fists and my toes curled as he rocked inside of me. Slow, deep, like I felt the walls inside of me might bust open. I uncurled my hands. Curled them again. Dug them into his skin. Squeezed the bed sheets between my fists.

When we were finished the lights gutted out. I rolled off the bed and searched for my clothes in the grass, in the dark. The singing grass picked up its song again, its howling song. I dressed.

"I can't stay together for long," he said.

"You came here just to take my virginity?" I asked.

"Of course not," he said. "I have business to take care of."

"Why were you buried in those jars?" I asked. "What's going to happen to you?"

"Don't worry about it, baby," he said.

He left.

The girl stood behind me.

"I know who you are," I said.

"No need to say it."

"What do I do now?"

"Go home and write about it," she said, and she left once more.

I didn't have to look back to know that the artist was behind me. I felt his cool shadow, his breath, the heart overworked from too many years of smoking cigarettes. The artist as tragic hero, I thought, burnt up and buried in jars. There's nothing more typical.

"Autumn, what's wrong?"

"Nothing. It doesn't matter anyways," I said.

A sickening vertigo overcame me. I fell in the grass before he could catch me, my head spinning. I heaved and my spine buckled. I vomited up the quivering cougar heart at his feet.

Acknowledgments

Special thanks to all the people who've stopped on a snowy evening to share the midnight road – including John Skipp, William Marsden, Lux Lubrano, Geordan Christian, Garrett Cook, Jeremy Maddux, Clara Suedmeier, Melissa Stowell, Robert Freeling, that one homeless guy with a friendly dog outside of the QT in Guthrie, and the girl I hugged for ten minutes in the parking lot of a music festival.

About the Author

Autumn Christian is a fiction writer who lives in the dark woods with poisonous blue flowers in her backyard and a black deer skull on her wall. She is waiting for the day when she hits her head on the cabinet searching for the popcorn bowl and all consensus reality dissolves.

She's been a freelance writer, a game designer, a cheese producer, a haunted house actor, and a video game tester. She considers Philip K. Dick, Ray Bradbury, Katie Jane Garside, the southern gothic, and dubstep as main sources of inspiration.

INDIEGOGO CAMPAIGN HALL OF FAME THANKS!!!

Michael Arnzen * David S. Atkinson * David Bridges * Natalie Briggs * John Bruni * Bob Brustman * Brian Bubonic * Hugo Camacho * Maraluce Catherine * RJ Cavender * Chad * Colleen The Tax Queen Cassidy * Mike Christian * John Wayne Comunale * N.C. Christopher Couch * Kyle Dare * Jarrid Deaton * Etienne Deforest * Hollie DeFrancisco * Robert Devereaux * Mr. T Duke * Frank Edler * Scott Eubanks * Karl Fischer * Dan Fisk * Constance Ann Fitzgerald * Rebecca "Soup" Franich * Rodney Gardner * His Majesty Eirik Gumeny, Lord of the Fly Girls * James Henry Hall * Jane Hamilton * Brad C. Hodson * Steven M Irwin * Jeremy Robert Johnson * Shawn Jones * Andrew Kasch * Ed Kemper * Jan Kozlowski * James Frederick Leach * Sean Leonard * Chin Li * Michael Ling * Kevin Lintner * Jonathan Maberry * Anton Major * Josh Spicoli Martens * Tracie McBride * Brian McClain * Nick Mozak * Charles Austin Muir * Sauda Namir * CS Nelson * Aaron Nemoyten * Michael Noe * Kit O'Connell * Marnie Olson * J David Osborne * Nicholaus Patnaude * Charles Pinion * Teresa Pollack * Scott Rabin * Martin Roberts * Michael Allen Rose * ryanrockshard * Tiffany Scandal * Tanya Semmons * Eric Seigel * Greg Sisco * Bix Skahill * Rick Slater * Virginia Slater * Curt Sobolewski * Kevin Strange * Deana Uutela * Kerry Vail * Matthew Vaughn * Marvin P Vernon * Grant M. Wamack Jr. * Tabitha Warrick * Ian Welke * Rick Westbrock * Frances Winkler * Mandy Zeller

9 781621 052104